Tyndale House Publishers, Inc.
Carol Stream, Illinois

7

. Friendly Foal *.*

DANDI DALEY MACKALL

Visit Tyndale's exciting Web site for kids at www.tyndale.com/kids and the Winnie the Horse Gentler Web site at www.winniethehorsegentler.com.

You can contact Dandi Daley Mackall through her Web site at www.dandibooks.com.

The Tyndale Kids logo is a trademark of Tyndale House Publishers, Inc.

Friendly Foal

Designed by Jacqueline L. Nuñez

Edited by Ramona Cramer Tucker

For manufacturing information regarding this product, please call 1-800-323-9400.

ISBN 978-0-8423-8723-1, mass paper

Printed in the United States of America

17   16   15   14
11   10   9   8   7

For the Medina County Career Center
Animal Care Program.
Thanks for passing along your
gift and love for animals.
Our animals are in great hands!

Chapter 1

A rare streak of sunlight poked through the barn slats and made the new black filly glow. Tiny frost clouds puffed from her nostrils as she stared, wide-eyed, at me across the stall.

I held out the bottle of goat's milk to her. "Come on. I'm not going to hurt you," I pleaded.

But the orphan foal ducked behind my horse Nickers and stood alert, her long, knobby-kneed legs stretched, giraffe-style.

I gave up and rested my head against my white Arabian's neck. "We've got to get that foal to trust me, Nickers," I whispered. I breathed in her horsey warmth and could have fallen asleep right there.

Since the birth of the foal on Christmas Eve, I'd spent three nights and three days in the barn, making sure she got the bottled colostrum, or first milk, she needed to survive. Now I wanted to get her used to goat's milk, the next best thing to mare's milk. Annie Goat was on loan to me from Granny Barker. As soon as the filly stopped being so scared of me, I planned to train her to nurse from the goat.

Annie was in no hurry to take on the foal. Ignoring us, she stood at the opposite end of the stall, munching hay. She looked like an old man chewing tobacco. I'd been bringing her into the stall with Nickers and the foal, hoping they'd all get used to each other. I needed the foal to nurse from Annie Goat.

Nickers licked the filly's neck and jaw. It made me proud, seeing the way my horse had adopted this scraggly orphan. The foal was born with four white stockings, a blaze on her forehead, and a black coat that was bushy and curly. She was beautiful but fragile. It was going to take everything I had to keep her healthy.

I stood on tiptoes to peek over Nickers at the foal.

The filly bolted as if I'd attacked her. She bumped the wall and nearly toppled over.

I stepped back to the stall door. "It's okay, girl. I'll stay away. I know how you feel."

She'd lost her mother, and the world didn't look friendly to her. I did know how the orphan felt. It had been two years since I'd lost *my* mom, and I still had trouble trusting humans.

I was born in Wyoming and had a pretty perfect life for my first ten years. My mom was the best horse gentler in the county, the state, maybe even the world. Everything I know about horses I learned from her. When she died, Dad moved my sister, Lizzy, and me from place to place until we ended up in Ashland, Ohio.

Things were working out, though. I think Mom would have been proud of me. I'd already become known as Winnie the Horse Gentler. And even though I'm only in seventh grade, people bring me their problem horses and actually pay me to gentle them.

That's kind of how I ended up with the foal's mother in my barn.

I glanced into the next stall and felt the tears press against my eyeballs as I remembered Gracie there. The dapple-gray mare had just shown up in my pasture one morning, an anonymous problem-horse gift for Winnie the Horse Gentler. I'd dubbed her "Amazing Grace."

But Gracie's only *problem* had been neglect. It had been a miracle that, sick as Gracie was, she held on until she delivered her foal.

My mind flashed me a photo of the old gray mare, lying in the hay, craning her neck to see her newborn foal. I have a photographic memory, so the details were all there—Gracie's big eyes glazed, the foal slick from birth, steam rising from the bed of hay.

Sometimes having a photographic memory isn't so great. Without my permission, my brain snaps pictures that etch their way deep into my mind forever, then pop up when I'd least like to see them. My brain has stored 100 photos of the accident that killed my mother. And now I have snapshots of Gracie dying too.

I shut my eyes, but the picture grew even sharper. Gracie died in my arms.

"Winnie? You okay?" Lizzy came up behind me. She didn't have a coat on, even though the temperature was below freezing.

"I still can't get the filly to trust me, Lizzy. I don't know what I'm doing wrong."

Mom used to say that the first 48 hours could

determine how well a foal got along with humans for the rest of its life. I'd passed the 48-hour mark and still couldn't get close to this filly.

"I'm sure you're not doing anything wrong. That little horse will come around!" Lizzy said, looking like a cheerleader. My sister is a year younger than me, but she's two inches taller. We both caught Mom's dark hair and lean build, but Lizzy dodged the freckles. "Just give her time. She'll see what a terrific friend Winnie Willis can be!"

Lizzy seemed to be glancing around the barn for something. "Geri hasn't come by, has she?" she asked, picking up Churchill, a giant gray cat that belongs to our friend Catman Coolidge. The cat rubbed his smushed-in, flat face against Lizzy's neck.

"Geri? Nope."

Geri is Lizzy's best friend. My sister loves all things lizard, and Geri is a frog nut. Sometimes I admit I'm a little jealous at how easily Lizzy makes great friends. If she got that from our mom, I guess I dodged it. Horses are so much easier to get along with than humans.

I put another fleck of hay in the hay net for

Nickers to play with. Nelson, my barn cat and Churchill's son, got in on the action and hopped to the feed trough, where he could paw at the hay net with his one white paw. "I thought Geri was coming over to spend the night."

"She is. We're supposed to work on her frog palace. Did I tell you she got a salamander for Christmas? I can't wait to see him! Salamanders really rock, you know? They shed their skins and sometimes eat the old skin for nutrients. And when it's cold—"

"Lizzy," I interrupted. Once she gets going, she talks faster than a trotter trots. *Somebody* has to stop her. "Did you come out here for something?" My sister usually stays as far away from horses as she can. She'll gladly hug spiders and toads and bugs, but she won't even touch Nickers.

Lizzy smacked her forehead with the heel of her hand. "Telephone! For *you!*"

"Me?" I almost never get phone calls. Except from Hawk, Victoria Hawkins, who was still in Florida visiting her dad. But Hawk had been calling at night.

"Sorry." Lizzy set down Churchill. "I can't believe I forgot the phone call! Duh to me. It's a girl. At first I thought it was Geri. But I think it might be Sal."

I doubted it. Sal, Salena Fry, is in most of my seventh-grade classes, and we get along okay. But she's buddies with Summer Spidell and the popular kids. Summer and I got off on the wrong foot the first time we met, when I was shoveling manure in her dad's fancy stable. I guess you could say we've pretty much stayed on the wrong foot since then.

Lizzy and I plowed through the snow toward the house. Our yard looked a hundred times better snow-covered. You couldn't even see the broken toasters, rolls of wires, and other machine parts Dad keeps around for his inventions and for repairing stuff. Snow had turned the tallest junk into white statues.

Once inside I kicked off my boots and ran to the kitchen phone, hoping the mystery caller was still there. "Hello?"

"Sal, she's here! On the phone!" The voice on the line sounded familiar, but it wasn't Sal. And whoever it was wasn't talking to me. She was screaming away from the phone.

"Hello?" I said again. "Who's this?"

"Uh . . . um . . . it's *going* to be Sal." Then

away from the phone, she screamed, "Sal! You have to come right now! I'm not holding the phone any longer. I mean it!"

"Geri?" I was pretty sure I recognized her voice. "Are you at Sal's house?"

Lizzy was sticking a tray of cookies into the oven. She stopped and frowned at me.

"Uh . . . hi, Winnie. How are you?"

"What are you doing over there, Geri? Lizzy has been—"

"Oops . . . here's Sal!"

The phone shuffled and clattered. Then another voice came over the line. "Winnie? Man, am I glad you're there! I thought you'd never get to the phone."

"Sal? What's Geri doing at your house?"

"I can't understand you, Winnie."

No wonder. There was a lot of commotion going on in the background at Sal's house, and Sal wasn't so easy to understand either. But I knew my voice wasn't helping. I always sound hoarse. Lizzy says it's exotic and she wishes she had my voice, but I think my words sound like they're filtered through gravel.

I cleared my throat, for all the good it would do me, and asked again why Geri was at Sal's.

"Nathan," Sal answered.

"Nathan?" Sal's brother is in sixth grade, like Lizzy and Geri. I'd only seen him a couple of times, but I could picture him. The first time I'd seen Nathan and Lizzy had introduced him as her buddy, Nate, I'd had to fight to keep from laughing. Sal's pretty out-there, with her wild jewelry and ever-changing hair colors. I'd expected her little brother to have tattoos and a shaved head. But Nathan looked like a regular kid—short dark hair, normal clothes, just a little on the chunky side.

Now I glanced at Lizzy. She looked as confused as I felt.

"If you ask me," Sal said, "Geri's got a king-size crush. And I don't think Nathan even knows what's up. Guys." The phone clanked again. Then Sal shouted, "Keep your socks on, Gram! I'm coming!" This was followed by so much noise on the other end of the line that I had to hold the phone away from my ear to keep from going deaf.

The phone rattled again, and Sal shouted, "Winnie, I'm coming right over!"

"You are?" The last time—the *only* time—Sal had come over, she'd acted like our entire house should have been condemned. She'd made her escape as fast as she could.

"Gram and I have a job for you. For Christmas she—" There was shuffling, then a *bang*, as if she'd dropped the phone. "All right! All right! I said I'm coming!" More shuffling, and Sal was back on the line. "Don't go anywhere! Stay right where you are! I'll explain everything when I get there. I need you desperately, Winnie Willis!"

I hung up the phone and tried to imagine why Sal would ever need me. What kind of job could she and her grandmother possibly have for me? It's no secret that Dad, Lizzy, and I are barely getting by. Dad used to be a big insurance boss in Laramie, Wyoming. But in Ashland, he's just Odd Job Willis, a not so great handyman and part-time inventor.

Maybe Sal thought I was Junior Miss Odd-Job Willis. Maybe she wanted me to shovel walks. Do her laundry. Clean her room.

The oven door slammed shut. Lizzy set the timer, which Dad had rewired to make it moo like a cow when it went off. Just another example of his helpful inventions.

"Did Geri say if she's still coming over?" Lizzy asked.

I shook my head. "Sal is, though. She claims she has a job for me." I watched Lizzy shove her hair back into a ponytail that looked tons better than my hair does after I've really worked on it.

"Did you know Geri and Sal's brother were . . . *together*?" I began. "I mean, last time I heard Sal mention Nathan, she said he couldn't stop talking about the donut squares you brought in for Geri's birthday and the Valentine sandwiches you made for everybody when it wasn't even Valentine's Day."

Lizzy grinned. "Nate loves to eat, all right." She glanced at the tray of green salamander cookies cooling on the counter. "So Geri didn't say if she's still coming? I made a lot of cookies. I'm calling them Salamander Mint. Maybe Madeline and Mason will come over and help us eat them."

"Or you could take Madeline a doggie bag . . . a *salamander* bag?" I suggested.

Madeline Edison is Dad's *friend*. She's an inventor too. She's pretty weird, although Dad seems to like her.

"Winnie," Lizzy scolded, "I think Madeline is

really trying to fit in. I know you *love* having Mason around. Besides, shouldn't he be helping you take care of that baby horse?"

"True," I admitted.

Madeline's son, Mason, has a condition, like autism, that makes him disappear inside himself sometimes, like he's not even there. I kind of envy that. It's what I feel like doing myself at least once a day. Only if *I* disappear, I'm taking Nickers with me.

I did want Mason to get used to the foal, and vice versa. But the foal wasn't even used to me yet. And I'm not always sure what Mason's going to do. Once I saw him close his eyes in the middle of watching cartoons. And for the next three minutes he screamed louder and louder. Then he just stopped and went back to the cartoon show.

Lizzy smiled at me, with the deep smile that reminds me of our mom. "You know, Winnie, giving that foal to Mason was about the nicest thing I've ever seen anybody do. I wish I had a picture of his face when you told him the foal was his."

Lizzy crumbled something into the lizard condo dad had invented for her collection.

Larry the Lizard stuck out his snout and gobbled up whatever Lizzy had dropped in.

"So what did you name the baby horse?" Lizzy asked.

"I haven't yet. I want Mason to name her."

Back in Wyoming Mom and I had worked out a system of dubbing horses with temporary names. That way it wouldn't be so hard on us when the horses went back to their owners. It hadn't worked, though. We were always sad to see any horse leave.

Still, I'd fallen into the same naming game since I'd become Winnie the Horse Gentler. First there was my Nickers, who used to be called Wild Thing. Then there was Grant's horse, Eager Star. Then Bold Beauty and Midnight Mystery. I used to call Towaco, Hawk's Appaloosa, Unhappy Appy. Before Gracie had her foal, I'd dubbed her Gift Horse.

And in my head I'd already found a fake name for the foal: Friendly Foal.

The timer *moo*ed, and Lizzy pulled out the pan of cookies.

She'd gone to so much work for Geri. "I can't believe Geri's doing this to you, Lizzy."

Lizzy smiled over at me as she poked a salamander to see if he was done. "You mean not coming over?" She set the cookie sheet on a dish towel. "Well, she should have called. But I'm not so surprised that she's over there with Nate. I kind of thought Geri had a crush on him, even though she claimed she didn't."

If I'd been Lizzy, I would have been fighting mad. I guess I got the freckles *and* the temper.

I checked out the kitchen clock. "Sal should have been here by now. What kind of a job do you think she's talking about, Lizzy?"

Lizzy was pulling things out of the fridge. "Didn't you ask her?"

"Kind of." I tried to remember what Sal had said exactly. Unfortunately, I don't have a *phonographic* memory. I couldn't replay the conversation. "But I'll tell you one thing. I'm not doing anything stupid for her. I wouldn't put it past Summer to put Sal up to this. She'll probably want me to shine her shoes or clean under her bed."

I thought about the first time Summer's dad, Spider Spidell, hired Odd-Job Willis to fix some broken halters for the horses in his fancy Stable-Mart. Nothing pleased him. Dad had to redo those halters four times, and Mr. Spidell still complained.

"Help Winnie calm down and know what you want her to do about Sal," Lizzy said. She looked like she was talking to one of the doughy salamanders, but she was talking to God. She prays as easily as a Tennessee Walking Horse walks.

I still hadn't taken off my barn coat, and my back was starting to sweat. "I better go out to the barn and wait. If Sal comes to the house, send her out, okay?"

"Sweet," Lizzy said. She wrapped a salamander in a napkin and handed him to me.

It smelled minty. We still had our Christmas tree up, but it didn't smell as evergreen minty as the salamander cookie.

"Thanks, Lizzy." I headed for the door. "Don't forget to send Sal!"

In the barn, I waited for Sal.

And waited.

And waited.

I fed the foal almost 16 ounces of Annie's

milk. But it was a struggle, probably worse because I was getting so irritated with Sal. And the more I thought about Geri hanging out with Nathan while my sister was waiting on *her*, the madder I got.

I almost had to wrestle the foal to keep her with me while she was bottle-nursing.

It was getting dark enough to turn on the barn light. I finished chores, mucked, raked, and checked supplies. I'd just about given up on Sal, when I heard the crunch of tires on snow, followed by the squeal of brakes.

I made it outside in time to see Sal leap from a bright red van as it pulled up behind our cattle truck.

"Over here, Sal!" I shouted, waving.

She turned and came jogging toward the barn. Sal was wearing a green quilted ski jacket and mittens the size of Georgia and Alabama. Black boots came to her knees, which was a good thing because she was wearing a miniskirt. Green fuzzy earmuffs couldn't hide the new purple stripe in her red hair. The stripe matched her eyeliner and the giant hoop earrings that dangled as she ran.

"What's up?" I hollered.

"I've got a job for you," Sal said, blowing into her mittens.

I wondered if Summer Spidell could be hiding in the van, spying to see my expression when Sal asked me to dig for fishing worms or brush her teeth or whatever.

"I'm pretty busy with an orphan foal, Sal," I said.

"Winnie! This is a *real* job." She kept glancing back at the van like it was her getaway vehicle.

I couldn't see who was driving, but someone raced the engine. The van shook. Then the motor cut out, and a woman sprang out the driver's door. She had boots and a miniskirt like Sal's. Only her ski jacket was red. Red earmuffs covered short black hair.

"Is that your mom?" I asked, realizing that I'd never seen either of Sal's parents. Hawk had told me Sal's parents were divorced, but they both lived in Ashland.

"Graham Cracker." Or at least that's what I thought Sal said. "She's my grandmother, *not* my mother," she explained. "Mom's maiden name was Cracker. So my grandmother is Gram Cracker."

I couldn't believe the pretty woman tiptoeing

toward us through the snow was anybody's grandmother. Her long earrings sparkled, and her lipstick matched her red coat.

"Wh-what's your *grandmother—*"

"I don't have time for this, Winnie," Sal interrupted, sounding as impatient as if *I'd* kept *her* waiting all afternoon. "Gram Cracker lives on the other end of town, County Road 1150. Both of my parents took off over Christmas, so I've been stuck at Gram's. This whole thing is *her* idea."

"What whole thing?" I asked.

I think Sal might have been about to answer me when a giant *thump* sounded from the van. It shook again, as if pounded by ocean waves.

Gram Cracker yelled something I won't repeat. Then she hurried back to the van and disappeared inside it.

"Who else is in that van, Sal?" I asked. Maybe Summer had brought the entire popular group with her for the big laugh. "What's this job you want me to do?"

Sal sighed, like she was tired of trying to explain something to an idiot. "Gram Cracker gave me a horse for Christmas."

"A horse! You're kidding! Wow! That's terrific.

What breed? Not that it matters. *Any* horse is great. Oh, Sal, you must be so excited!"

But Sal didn't look excited. "Yeah, right."

The horn honked.

Sal glared at the van.

The horn honked again.

"I'm coming!" Sal shouted. "The woman has the patience of a tadpole."

My mind was racing. Sal had a horse, and they wanted *me* to train it! I could sure use the extra money. I'd spent January's budget on colostrum and vet bills for Friendly Foal. I'd always thought Sal could be a friend, if it weren't for Summer Spidell getting in the way. Maybe if I trained her horse . . .

Sal had started picking her way back to the van.

"Wait, Sal!" I called after her. "When can you bring your horse over?"

Sal laughed. "Now!"

She stopped where she was, then waved her arms over her head. "Now, Gram!"

Gram Cracker flattened herself against the driver's door. Then she shoved open the sliding rear door.

For a minute, nothing happened.

Gram looked scared, as if she expected a tiger to burst from the backseat.

The van shook again.

And as I watched, stunned, breathless, out jumped a horse!

I stared across the snowy yard at the tiny gelding, who pranced through the snow as if he didn't want to get his hooves wet. He was a black-and-white miniature, no more than seven hands high—29 inches, tops. But his body was perfectly proportioned, not like Shetland ponies or most miniatures. No big pony head or stubby legs. This horse looked exactly like a *horse*—lean, with a fine head and delicate legs. It was like somebody had taken a Pinto Thoroughbred or Arabian and shrunk it.

"Still think every breed is so terrific?" Sal asked, sounding like *she* didn't.

"Are you kidding? He's wonderful, Sal! What a cutie!" As I said it, he kicked up his heels, then

23

reared and pawed the air like a ferocious stallion. I laughed out loud.

"Yeah," Sal muttered. "Real funny. Like I'm going to get a lot of use out of this midget."

Gram Cracker darted to us, as if for protection. "You're the horse girl? So what's the matter with this horse? Is it a freak? What's wrong with it?"

I couldn't take my gaze off the horse. "He's perfect! You're so lucky. He's a miniature, but he's got to be a Falabella horse, not a pony."

I pointed to the gelding, now pawing snow like he could dig himself an escape tunnel. "See those tiny hooves and that absolutely perfect conformation?"

Gram Cracker elbowed Sal, who stood a head taller than her grandmother. Sal nearly fell over from the force. Gram Cracker reminded me of a spirited Tarpan pony, small but solid and not to be messed with. "I told you I picked out a great Christmas gift for you!" Gram said. "But *no!* Nothing is good enough for Salena."

Sal glared at her grandmother. "*You* didn't pick that thing out! Raoul did." She turned to me to explain. "Raoul is her boyfriend."

"*Ex*-boyfriend," Gram corrected. "Never accept the love of an Argentine caballero."

"Argentina?" I repeated. "Then I'm right! It's got to be a Falabella. That's where they come from. I've never actually seen one, just pictures in books and on the Internet."

Gram Cracker frowned at me and patted my head. "Laryngitis? You should get out of the cold, girl."

Sal laughed. "She always talks like that, Gram."

I felt my face heat up and my freckles pop out.

"You should get that taken care of," Gram insisted. She turned to the little horse, who was busy sniffing the snow. "Shouldn't you catch it?"

"Oh yeah. Sorry." I'd been so awed by the horse that I hadn't even thought about what to do with him.

I started toward him. "Hey, little fella. Let's see about getting you in the barn."

He jerked up his head, his ears pointing straight up. Then he snorted and trotted off in the opposite direction.

Behind me Gram Cracker said, "I thought you

told me that girl has some kind of special powers with horses."

"That's what Grant said, Gram. I wanted to take the little monster to Summer's dad's stable, but they were all full."

It didn't help my ego to know that Sal's first choice had been Spidells' Stable-Mart. Their stable looks fancier than mine, but horses like mine better.

Still, it was nice to know that Grant said I was good with horses. Grant Baines is probably the most popular guy in our middle school. I'd helped him train his barrel horse. I guess he and Summer are going out. At least Summer thinks they are. Poor Grant.

I moved toward the little horse again. He darted away from me, faster than the first time. But at least he wasn't trying to run away. If I stayed with him, he'd let me come up to him eventually.

"Winnie!" Sal shouted. "You want us to help trap him? That's what *we* had to do."

I shook my head no. No wonder the horse wouldn't let me near him. Sal and Gram must have scared him good by trapping him.

"Tell her we haven't got all night," Gram Cracker said.

Sal obeyed. "Winnie, we haven't got all night!"

"Come on, boy," I coaxed, moving in again.

He walked away from me, then stopped. I followed, moving from side to side, so he'd see me no matter where he turned. Sooner or later he'd get the idea that I was everywhere and he couldn't lose me. Then he'd quit trying.

Only I needed to catch him *sooner*, rather than *later*.

"Horse girl!" Gram Cracker yelled.

Startled, the gelding broke into a canter and raced past me.

"I have an aerobics class in 10 minutes!" Gram complained. "Sal and I caught that wild, spotted pony faster than this, chasing him into a corner. Just chase him!"

Gram turned to Sal but didn't lower her voice. "I thought you said Winnie the Whatever was good at this."

My stomach threatened to return Lizzy's minty salamander. What if Sal and her grandmother decided I couldn't handle this horse?

What if they took him back? Or sent him back to Argentina?

I closed in behind the gelding. "Come on, boy. My reputation is on the line here. And so is your American citizenship."

"Winnie! Brian's waiting for me at Pizza-Mart right now!" Sal screamed.

"And I told Nate I'd pick him up from the bowling alley before I go to aerobics!" Gram complained.

I had to catch this horse. They weren't going to wait.

He trotted by me, heading in the direction of the barn.

"Gram, let's just go and let Winnie worry about it!" Sal said.

"Look, Sal," Gram Cracker snipped back, "if the horse girl can't even *catch* the horse, how can she train him?"

I *had* to do it. I couldn't wait any longer.

He loped in front of the barn. He was two feet from the open barn door.

"Heee-yah!" I charged him, waving my arms. "Get!"

He stopped short, sliding in the snow and turning white-rimmed eyes on me.

I swallowed, knowing I didn't want to do this but not knowing what else to do. "Get on in!" I shouted. I shuffled my feet and advanced on him.

He backed away from me, his rump heading straight for the barn. I ran at him. He pivoted and, with nowhere else to run, trotted into the barn.

I hurried after him and blocked his exit with my body.

"Finally!" Gram hollered. "All right then!"

I felt sick inside. If I'd witnessed anybody else handle a horse like I just had, I would have jumped all over them.

Sal came over, but Gram was already making her way back to the van.

"You've got two minutes, Sal!" Gram shouted. "Then I'm leaving with or without you!"

"You know what to do with it, right?" Sal asked. "I mean, if there's anything you *can* do with a horse that small. You can't even ride it."

"Falabellas make great pets, Sal."

"Right. It bites, kicks, and jumps up on its hind legs. Great pet."

"He's just scared." And I sure hadn't helped that.

"Whatever." Sal frowned at the barn. "You do

have a stall for him, though, right? At least he doesn't take up much space."

"I'll put him next to Nickers and the foal."

The foal. She was still my most important job. What was I doing, taking on another problem horse, when I hadn't even started imprinting Friendly yet?

"Listen, Sal, I'm really glad you trust me with your horse. And I want to help . . . besides the fact that I can use the money."

"Cool. We're tight then." She made a move to leave.

"But you're going to have to help me, Sal. I have this foal to work with. And anyway, this one is *your* horse. You're the one we want him to get used to."

"He hates me."

"He doesn't hate you, Sal. You just need to spend time with him. Time and patience." I could almost hear my mom saying that. Maybe I *did* have a phonographic memory.

Sal stamped her feet and blew into her mittens again. "Okay, okay, okay. I'll be patient. I gotta go, though. Right now!"

As if on cue, the van's horn sounded.

Sal turned to leave.

"I mean it, Sal! I need you here. Tomorrow morning! Early!"

"Early on vacation is 11 o'clock," she said, making her getaway.

"Okay. But be here at 11 sharp! Tomorrow."

Sal kept going, but gave me a one-mitten wave, which I took as an okay.

I watched her climb into the van and slam the door. Then I thought of something. "Sal!" I yelled, stumbling over a snowdrift as I ran to the van. "Wait!"

Gram Cracker backed up the van, then pulled it forward, as if she hadn't heard me.

I made it to the street just as she was ready to pull out. "What's his name? What's your horse's name?" I shouted.

Gram rolled down her window. "Amigo," she answered, cutting the wheel for a sharp turn around.

Sal leaned forward from the passenger seat. "Funny, huh? *Amigo*, as in 'friend'? Like that munchkin and I could ever be friends."

Gram gunned it. Tires spun. Snow sprayed. And the red van swerved toward town, minus one small horse.

I hurried back to the barn, where I found the

tiny, spotted horse shivering at the far end of the stallway.

Amigo.

It didn't take a horse gentler to see that the little gelding wanted to be friends with me about as much as Sal did.

Chapter 4

It was just after seven that same night, but it felt a lot later as I edged down the stallway toward Amigo. Nickers gave a friendly nicker, and I hoped Amigo would get the message. Maybe he would trust my horse, even though he clearly didn't trust me. If this kept up, people would have to start bringing their horses to *Nickers* the Horse Gentler.

Slowly I closed the gap between Amigo and me. "It's okay, Amigo." I tried to keep my voice low and easy, but I was too wound up from Gram and Sal.

The little gelding shied away from me.

I reached out for him, but he flinched. "I'm so sorry, Amigo." I had to get him to his stall. I grabbed for his halter.

His head shot out, and he bit me.

"Ow!" I jerked my hand away. He'd caught me a good one on my upper arm, biting right through my jacket.

Amigo's back twitched as if he had a swarm of flies after him. He cowered closer to the back wall, waiting for me to punish him.

"I'm not going to hurt you. I know you're just scared." I'd need to teach him not to bite. But it would have to wait until I gained his trust.

Carefully I touched his withers, out of reach of those surprisingly sharp teeth. My arm still stung, hurting more as my jacket rubbed against the sore spot.

Amigo flinched, but I didn't pull away. I scratched him, lightly trailing my fingers over his withers, at the base of his white mane.

He trembled but didn't shy away. As I kept it up, I felt him relax a little. "That's it," I whispered.

Nickers nickered. The foal made her muffled squeal. I was overdue getting her goat's milk. I'd have to milk Annie again.

"Easy, Amigo," I urged, turning back to him. He tried to jerk his head from me, but I got a good grip on his rhinestone-studded halter.

It wasn't easy, but I put Amigo into the stall next to Nickers. Nickers tried to be friendly and snort hello over the stall divider, but Amigo wouldn't have it. He turned his back on us and moved to the farthest corner of the stall. His neck drooped, and his tail was tucked between his legs.

It was going to take a lot to win him over.

Annie Goat fought me while I milked her. I barely got enough for one bottle. I kept hoping Eddy Barker would stop by. Maybe he knew one of Granny Barker's secrets about getting along with her goat.

Barker is in seventh grade with me. His whole family—which includes his five brothers—got to see the foal's birth on Christmas Eve. The next day Barker brought Annie Goat over, on loan from Granny Barker. Granny B claims her husband was the best African-American farmer in the Midwest. She'd moved into town to live with her son and family, but she refused to sell the farm, which is where she'd been keeping Annie.

I could have used Barker's help. I could have used M's help too. M, a pretty unique friend of mine who goes by a letter instead of a name, had helped me deliver the foal. He'd helped me feed Friendly the first two days too, when we had to give her a little bit of colostrum every hour or so. But M's parents had taken him along on one of their Habitat for Humanity trips. I figured that, about now, M and his parents were hammering shingles on a little house in Cleveland.

I finally got the whole bottle of milk down Friendly, but she struggled so much she made Annie look like Miss Congeniality. I had to admit I was doing some struggling of my own. The best tool any horse person has is patience, but I kept ending up shorthanded.

I walked over to Nickers, and she rested her head on my shoulder so we could talk eye-to-eye. I scratched her dish jowl and saw myself in her big brown eyes. "You know, girl, Lizzy has been after me to make my New Year's resolutions this year. I think I just thought of my first resolution: I, Winnie Willis, resolve to be more patient."

Nickers exhaled, blowing gently in my face. It's the way horses greet each other. Native Americans used to greet their horses by blowing into their nostrils. My mom taught me to do the same thing.

I returned Nickers' greeting, feeling myself calm down for the first time all day.

Something bumped against the barn, right outside the stall.

"Who's there?" I shouted, my calm quick-freezing, then shattering into pieces. "Who's out there?"

Nickers backed away from me to hover over the foal. Why had I shouted like that?

Annie didn't like the shouting either. She hopped on her back legs and hooked her front hooves over the stable door, as if she might try scaling the wall.

My nerves had sprung back that fast. I could have climbed the wall with her.

"Down, Annie!" I shouted. But, of course, the shouting just made her worse. She tried harder to scramble over the door. I had to lift her hooves off to get her down.

Something thumped from outside again.

"Who's out there?" I called.

A cat meowed. Then I heard purring. And more purring. So much purring that it sounded like a humming band.

And I had my answer.

"Hey, Catman! Be right out." I took the back stall door to the paddock.

Just as suspected, I found Calvin "Catman"

Coolidge sitting in the snow outside Nickers' stall. His long legs were totally covered by a swarm of cats, including Churchill, Nelson, and a pure white longhair I was pretty sure I'd never seen before . . . although Catman owns about a thousand cats, and I might have missed one. My sister calls Catman the "Pied Piper of Cats."

He was staring at the sky, his long blond hair blowing like a flag in the icy breeze. The white cat snuggled inside Catman's camouflage army jacket. Catman would have made a great hippie, like back in the 60s. Lizzy says he's living history, but he's only in eighth grade.

"New cat?" I asked, easing down into the snow next to him. Shivering, I stuffed my straggling hair under my stocking cap and tried to tuck my jacket under me.

Catman, on the other hand, wore no hat or gloves but showed no signs of being cold. Maybe it was the cats curled up on him like a fur coat.

"Rice," Catman answered. He and Lizzy are opposites when it comes to talking. If Lizzy's a racing Thoroughbred, Catman's an old Clydesdale, not about to take a step if a step's not needed.

"The white cat's name is Rice?" I asked.

Catman zipped up his jacket so only the cat's white furry head stuck out. "David Rice Atchinson. Rice, for short."

I got ready for another history lesson. Every time Catman names a new cat, I learn something I never got in history class. "You gotta tell me who David Rice Atchoo's son was."

"Atchinson," Catman corrected. "U.S. president. For a day."

"No way!" Maybe I couldn't still name all the presidents like we had to in fifth grade, but at least I would have recognized the name.

Catman used his index finger to push his gold wire-rimmed glasses up his long nose. Even in the dark, his eyes shone true blue. "Zachary Taylor succeeded James Polk at noon on March 4, 1849."

I recognized Taylor's and Polk's names.

"But it was a Sunday," Catman continued. "And Zach refused to take the oath on the Sabbath. Far out, true? So under the Succession Act of 1792, Senator Atchinson, pro tempore of the Senate, took the oath and became president for a day. Groovy, huh? The new prez dug being top dog so much, he gave all his buddies cabinet seats."

I wondered if Ms. Mertz, my fifth-grade teacher, had any idea.

Hundreds of bright silver dots were sprinkled across the black sky, like heaven's private snow. Catman kept staring up at the same spot.

"What are you looking at?" I asked.

"Polaris," he answered.

"Huh?"

"North Star."

I leaned toward him, trying to follow his exact line of vision. But I couldn't tell the North Star from the South Star.

Note to self: Is there a South Star? And if not, why not?

Catman pointed straight through the branches of a big oak tree. "Tip of the Little Dipper."

I followed his finger through the leafless *V* of the oak's trunk. Just a little to the left, I made out four stars in a crooked square, with more stars curved like a handle. "Is that it?"

Catman shook his head without taking his eyes off the sky. *"Big* Dipper. Follow the pointer stars, those two at the end of the Big Dipper's cup."

I let my eyes draw a line from the two stars, straight across the sky. The line led to a dim star that lay directly through the *V* of the oak tree. It looked like the tip of the Little Dipper. "That one?" I asked.

"Polaris," Catman answered.

Wilhemina, Catman's fat orange tabby, waddled from Catman's lap to mine, purred and rubbed her face on my arm, then hopped back.

Cats totally trust the Catman. Usually horses trust me the same way. And dogs trust Barker. It had been great hanging out with Catman and Barker when we moved to Ashland. We even share a part-time job at Pat's Pets, manning the Pet Help Line.

I fought off a yawn. I didn't have time for tired. "I better get going. If I don't at least do one imprinting lesson with the foal, I don't think I'll sleep tonight."

Catman finally looked down at me. He raised one eyebrow nearly to the top of his forehead, without even moving the other brow.

"Imprinting," I explained, "is touching the foal, handling her kind of like a mare would nuzzle her foal. Native Americans used to talk to horses *before* birth, then handle the foals all over the first few days after birth. That's imprinting—

showing foals that even though you're a human, you're a friend, and they can trust you."

"Far-out!"

"Not so far-out," I said. "I've hardly touched the foal. She's still scared of me."

An owl hooted.

Catman hooted back, holding up the two-fingered peace sign to the invisible bird. "Peace!" he called out.

Peace. Why couldn't I be more like Catman? More peaceful? A lot of *unpeaceful* things had happened in the past year, including too many fights with my dad, too much friction with his *friend* Madeline, and too many problems at school.

Note to self: New Year's Resolution #2: I, Winnie Willis, resolve to be more peaceful.

I leaned back and gazed at the sky. My arm had finally stopped hurting where Amigo bit it. Twinkling stars sent down sparkles across the snowy pasture. Bare branches made purple, wavy shadows on the glittering snow, patterns in dapple-gray, like Gracie.

I breathed in crisp, fresh air, earthy smoke from someone's chimney, Catman's musky smell, leather, and horse. Horse nickers from the barn blended with winter sounds—snow crunching, branches creaking and complaining, wind whistling through the eaves.

It was working. *Peace.* I was entering a new year, a peaceful year. Everything would go smooth as snow, starting right now. *Peace.* I could feel it in my bones.

Bam! Bam bam!

Inside, Annie Goat pawed the stall floor.

Bam! Bam! Bam!

The pawing turned into kicking. The stall door rattled as the goat's kicks grew louder.

I tried to ignore it. *Peace. Feel it in my bones.*

Nickers whinnied. She stamped the ground. A cat screeched. The goat cried.

Thump! ***Thud!***

Somebody screamed.

I jumped up. Cats flew in all directions.

I raced inside the barn just in time to see the stall door fly open under the goat's hooves.

"Annie!" I cried, jumping into the stall. Nickers and Friendly scuffled to the far corner.

"It's breaking out!" Madeline Edison's cry filled the barn.

"Winnie!" Dad shouted. *"Do something, for crying out loud!"*

I raced to the busted stall door, throwing myself between the charging Annie Goat and the screaming Madeline Edison.

Annie stopped and lowered her head. She pawed the ground like she was a bull getting set for the bullfight of her life.

I stared back at her, waiting, my mind racing. *Peace? Feel it in my bones?*

Note to self: Never trust your bones.

$\mathcal{L}$ couldn't help wondering if anyone had ever broken *all* of her New Year's resolutions before it even got to the new year. Or maybe they didn't count until New Year's Day?

Annie Goat's beady eyes locked onto me as she pawed the ground.

"My baby horse!"

I hadn't even seen Mason behind Madeline and Dad. He's small for seven, and his voice is as thin and wispy as his angel-blond hair.

I took my gaze off Annie to look over my shoulder for Mason.

Big mistake.

Annie charged.

Madeline shrieked.

"Stop that goat!" Dad shouted.

Bam! Amigo kicked *his* stall door.

Mason ran under my outstretched arm, stumbling past Annie and toward the foal.

"Don't, Mason!" I cried, jumping between Annie and Mason.

Mason lunged at the foal. He was just trying to hug her, but Friendly didn't know that.

Neither did Nickers. She snorted and flattened her ears back, warning off anybody who threatened *her* baby.

"Mason!" I yelled.

He bumped into the foal.

The foal, knocked off balance, plopped backward onto her rear end.

Nickers reared.

"Mason, get out!" I screamed. Forgetting all about Annie Goat, I ran after Mason.

Annie charged past me.

Stamping and shuffling went on behind me.

"Madeline!" Dad screamed.

I turned in time to see Annie and Madeline crash into each other like two battering rams. Annie won. Madeline's feet left the floor. She tumbled backward, flying into Dad. They both went down.

"Go, horsey!" Mason cried, as if he and the foal were the only ones in the barn.

The foal sat in the middle of the stall like an overgrown dog.

Mason stood on one leg next to the stunned foal.

It took me a second to figure out what he was doing. He was trying to mount. He wanted to ride Friendly!

Nickers, teeth bared, wasn't about to let that happen.

"Mason!" I shouted as loud as I could, "Get out of the way!" I grabbed for him. Missed. My elbow caught his shoulder.

He lost his balance.

And I shoved him away as Nickers raced beside the foal.

Mason plopped down in the straw bedding, just like the foal had done.

"You can't ride a baby horse, Mason!" My heart was pounding. My hands shook, and so did my voice. "You could have been hurt! You shouldn't have—!"

I stopped. The barn had grown silent, except for my screaming.

And Mason was still.

I peered through his thick glasses at blue eyes that had turned to ice. He sat perfectly motionless, his little legs sprawled in the exact position as when he'd landed.

I glanced up at Catman, who was biting his lower lip and staring down at Mason.

Nobody moved in the stallway. Even Amigo kept quiet in the next stall.

"I'm sorry, Mason," I said. "I know you didn't mean anything."

Mason didn't look at me. He didn't look at anything. His eyes were locked on nothingness. And he wasn't there.

"I-It's okay, Mason," I muttered. I knew better than to yell at him. It can take days—months even—for Mason to get over stuff. I'd worked hard to get him to trust me. My throat burned, and I wanted my words back.

The foal struggled to get up. It took two tries for her to push herself up on her wobbly hind legs. She and Nickers took off for the rear of the stall.

"See, Mason? She's fine." I squatted next to him.

Blank eyes stared out. He'd made his own escape.

"Is he all right?" Madeline called. It sounded like she was struggling to get up too. "I'm coming, Mason!"

That was the last thing I needed—Madeline Edison. She's more afraid of horses than Lizzy is.

"Come on, Mason," I said, lifting him off the ground. He's lighter than a sack of feed, but he felt stiff as a hay bale. It was like he didn't even know I was holding him.

Catman came over and took Mason from me. "Hey, little man. Let's split this scene." He hoisted Mason onto his shoulders and slipped out of the stall.

I took a deep breath and followed them.

In the stallway Dad was brushing straw off Madeline's pink ski pants.

She ran to meet Catman. "Are you all right, honey?" She lifted Mason from Catman's shoulders. Madeline Edison is very strong for somebody so skinny. Her stocking cap fell off, freeing bright red hair to sprout around her face. "You're safe now, Mason." Her voice trembled. "You didn't get hurt, did you, sweetie?"

Mason didn't answer. Now he stared toward the foal. He was shivering, his eyes wide as a frightened stallion's.

I glanced back at the foal. *She* was shivering, *her* eyes wide too, as she stared back at the little human who had tried to ride her.

They were squared off at each other, like boxers gone to separate corners to wait for the next round.

Madeline put Mason down, but he didn't go anywhere.

"I was afraid this whole business was a bad idea, Jack," she said to Dad, as if I weren't there.

"Well, we're all pretty rattled now, Madeline," Dad said, pulling a piece of straw out of her tangled red hair. "Why don't we go inside where it's warm, and we can talk about this calmly?"

Dad reached down and patted Mason on the back. "I'll bet we can talk Lizzy into making us hot chocolate. What do you think, Mason?"

Mason didn't answer.

"It's all my fault," I said. "I'm sorry. I didn't mean to yell. I just didn't want—" I stopped myself before I said *didn't want Mason to get hurt*. I knew that was exactly what Madeline worried about every single day—that Mason *would* get hurt.

I couldn't blame her.

Mason has a lot of problems. Something

happened to him when he was a baby, something Madeline won't talk about. And whatever it was hurt his brain. Neurological damage, Dad calls it. He says Madeline is trying not to be overprotective, but it's not easy.

"I know you mean well, Winnie," she said. Her mouth twitched. I think it was her way of trying to smile. She wiggled her nose, like she was about to sneeze but couldn't. It made my eyes water. "It's just that I can't have Mason around wild animals if—"

"Yeh-eh-eh-eh!" Annie let out a cry from somewhere outside the barn.

"Annie!" Between Mason and the foal I'd forgotten the crazy goat.

Dad stood by Madeline and Mason, looking like he was ready to fend off dragons.

I dashed out of the barn, around the corner, and—whack!—smack into Eddy Barker.

Barker had a squirmy black puppy in one hand and the goat in the other. "Lose something?" he asked.

"Barker!" I cried, taking Annie by the collar.

Eddy Barker may be the nicest person in Ashland, maybe in all Ohio. His wool mask was pushed back on top of his head. Thick black hair pushed through the eyes and nose holes.

"Your granny's goat is something else, Barker," I said, struggling to hold on to her.

Catman appeared. "Hey, man!" He lifted the dog from Barker's arms and held the puppy against his cheek. "Irene's?"

Barker nodded, meaning the puppy was one from Irene's litter. Barker had trained the chocolate Lab for his little brother Mark. When Irene had puppies, Mark got to keep one.

"Mark named him Zorro," Barker explained. "We're trying to get him used to people. Whenever he's not with Irene, one of us is holding him."

I elbowed Catman. "See? That's like imprinting. Getting him used to people."

Dad and Madeline wandered out of the barn with Mason between them.

"Hi, Mr. Willis! Ms. Edison! How are you doing, Mason?" Barker called.

Dad and Madeline waved at him, then made their way over to us.

Annie jerked to get away from me, but I held tight.

Catman showed Zorro to Mason, but Mason didn't even seem to notice the puppy.

"The little fella looks healthy, Eddy," Dad said, scratching Zorro's head.

"He's doing fine," Barker said. "I'm headed over to Pat's Pets to noseprint him."

"Did he say *noseprint* him?" Madeline asked Dad.

Catman gave Barker the dog back. Zorro wagged his little tail and licked Barker's chin.

"I take imprints of all our dogs' noses. Each noseprint is unique. No two alike. Like snowflakes." Barker stared up at Madeline. "What happened to your chin?"

I looked, and there on Madeline's chin was a big Snoopy Band-Aid. I couldn't believe I hadn't noticed it before. I must not have looked up far enough.

Catman slipped his arm around Annie's shoulders and stooped down to a frog position. "Chill, hairy dude. I'll escort you to your pad." Catman frog-walked Annie to the barn.

"Thanks, Catman!" I called after them.

I moved in for a better look at Madeline's Band-Aid.

She fingered the Band-Aid as if she'd forgotten it was there. "My invention."

"You invented the Band-Aid?" I asked. She

didn't seem rich. Someone who invented Band-Aids should be rich.

"The trampoline suit," Dad said, as if that explained everything.

Madeline's eyes got glassy, sort of like Mason's. "I've almost got it. A whole-body suit made of a synthetic I've come up with— bounceon. My manufacturing slogan is 'In the trampoline suit, falling is half the fun!'"

"It looks like a scuba-diving suit, but the bounceon makes you bounce. I've seen Madeline fall backward off a stepladder and bounce back to the first rung!" Dad was whispering, like this was top-secret stuff.

Madeline paced, dragging Mason along with her. She reminded me of a nervous American Saddle Horse yearling.

"I never should have gotten injured," she muttered. "Not from a frontal fall."

"Maybe if you made the bounceon thicker?" Dad ventured.

Madeline fingered her Snoopy Band-Aid as if she hadn't heard Dad. "I've got it! The bounceon! I need to make it thicker! And wear a better helmet with a chin strap."

It made me mad that she acted like thicker bounceon was *her* bright idea.

A horn beeped. I recognized the *ba-ru-ga* of the Barker Bus, an old yellow van that Mrs. Barker drives around, filled with Barker boys and dogs.

I wondered if Madeline knew my dad had invented the dog seat belts in that van.

Mrs. Barker waved and *ba-ru-ga*-ed again. She's so patient though, that even the horn honk sounded nice. Both she and Barker's dad teach at Ashland University exotic courses like art and African-American literature. But she still finds time to drive her kids to everything.

Catman returned from the barn. "Pat's?" he asked Barker.

"Sure," Barker answered. "We can work on the help line. She's open late tonight—holiday hours."

I hadn't been to Pat's Pets since before Christmas. "Tell Pat I'll come in early tomorrow for the horse e-mails." Sal wasn't coming until 11, so I'd have time to answer e-mails first.

Catman, Barker, and Zorro headed to the Barker Bus.

"I better go too," Madeline said.

"But . . . but I thought we were going in for hot chocolate," Dad stammered. "And you said you'd take a look at the golf buddy."

The golf buddy was Dad's latest invention. It was supposed to send out smoke signals so bad golfers wouldn't have to hunt for their balls. But judging by all of the charcoal golf balls lying around our house, Dad hadn't quite worked out the kinks yet.

I was just glad this invention didn't have the potential to make my personal life miserable—unlike the backward bike, which I pedal backwards to school and still get teased for. Or the singing watch that wouldn't take "off" for an answer, even during my English final. Or the self-tying shoelaces that wrecked my gym career.

Madeline leaned down and tightened the chin string on Mason's hood and stared at it, as if she'd never seen a hood before and was thinking of inventing one.

"Madeline," Dad started.

"Tomorrow morning. I'll come first thing. Right now I have to move on the new bounce-on formula. You understand, don't you?"

"Well, I suppose—"

"Less cotton. More gel . . ." She was muttering

to herself. She picked up Mason and jogged toward her van, with Mason staring back at us over her shoulder. She overtook Catman and Barker.

"Early, Madeline! Be here by eight!" Dad called.

"Will do!" Madeline yelled back without turning around.

Dad took giant steps to our house as Madeline and Mason piled into their van.

Catman and Barker climbed into the Barker Bus. Mrs. Barker rolled down her window and waved to me before pulling away from the curb.

I waved back as they made a U-turn in the street.

A bitter wind wrapped itself around me. And suddenly I was alone. Totally alone. On a cold, dark night.

I watched as Mrs. Barker drove off down the street, the Barker Bus growing smaller and the taillights dimmer and dimmer until they disappeared altogether.

And I couldn't keep myself from wondering what it would feel like to be driven by your mom anywhere, for something as little as noseprinting your pet.

ℒ finally dragged into the house after bedding down Amigo, Nickers, and Friendly Foal. Lizzy had green hot chocolate waiting for me and red candy that tasted like raspberries and radishes. I ate four pieces.

Geri hadn't come over, and she hadn't called.

"Do you have to go back out?" Lizzy asked, wrapping the candies individually so they looked like Hershey's Kisses.

"Not tonight." I couldn't remember the last time I'd slept in my own bed. "The foal won't need another feeding until 5 A.M. Besides, she'll rest better without me."

That was the truth. When I'd sprinkled fresh straw in the stalls, the filly had tried as hard as Amigo to stay out of my way.

Lizzy pulled up a chair. "You could use a good night's sleep."

Something banged from Dad's workshop off the kitchen.

"Poor Dad," Lizzy said. "He's been burning golf balls ever since Madeline left."

Dad stormed into the kitchen. Without even a glance at us, he filled a huge plastic glass with water and ran back to the workshop. I smelled smoke.

Lizzy sighed. "Hey, has Hawk called yet?"

Hawk had been great about phoning me from her dad's place in Florida. At school she mostly hangs out with Summer, Sal, Grant, and the other popular kids. We'd talked more on the phone during the past week than we had in person all year. Still, I couldn't wait for her to get back.

I yawned. "Nope. But I'd probably fall asleep on the phone anyway. Think I'll take a nice hot bath and climb into a real bed, Lizzy."

I was clean, dry, and dressed in pj's when Hawk called.

"Hi, Hawk. When are you coming home?"

She laughed. Hawk's laugh is refined, almost musical. It fits her real name, which is Victoria Hawkins. Summer and the kids at school call her Victoria.

"Father has not told me for certain when I'll be home. He will hire a professional to drive Towaco back, and I will fly. But I talked to Mother this morning, and she has it all arranged. Winnie, I am having *the* New Year's Eve party for our class. And, of course, you *have* to come!"

I'd never been to a real New Year's Eve party, not one with classmates. I've been to a lot of schools, and I haven't fit into any of them. "That's great, Hawk!"

"Summer and Sal will be there, of course," she continued. "And Grant and Brian said they could come."

Hawk had called me last. Still, she *was* inviting me. *Me,* to a party the popular kids would talk about for the rest of the year. I hated it when everybody at school went on and on about how great a party was, and I hadn't even known there *was* a party.

Hawk kept talking about tacos and yard-long sundaes. Then suddenly her tone changed. "I had wanted to have an entirely Native American theme."

"Great idea!" We both like the fact that she's Native American, although neither of her parents is into it.

"I thought it was a great idea as well," Hawk said, the energy draining from her voice. "Mother did not."

There was an awkward pause.

Then Hawk asked, "How is that Friendly Foal today, Winnie? Lizzy said you get to sleep inside tonight, so I assume the foal must be doing better?"

I filled Hawk in on Friendly and the Mini, but she already knew about Amigo from Sal. I also told her everything that had gone wrong with the foal *and* with Amigo.

"Just keep trying with Amigo," she said. "I don't think Sal is convinced that this horse is a great gift."

I thought I heard Hawk yawn. Then *I* yawned, wondering if yawns were contagious over the phone. We said good night.

I fell into bed and snuggled under the covers. I really did try to stay awake and pray about everything. But I'd barely gotten to the first "God bless . . ." when I dropped off.

I don't know what time it was when Lizzy sneaked in and her bedsprings creaked.

I was too tired to move. But I fought off sleep and hoped this would be one of Lizzy's pray-out-loud nights. I never know when Lizzy will talk to God out loud instead of in her head. I don't think even she knows. But I've come to wait for Lizzy's prayers. She prays like our mom did.

"Father," Lizzy whispered, and the room got so still that the whisper had the force of a shout. "I had a great day with you today. Thanks for helping me with those cookies and with my lizard."

Lizzy talked to God about Dad and Madeline and Mason. Then it was my turn.

"Thanks for Winnie. You did such a great job in the sister department. And I love that Hawk's being such a good friend to Winnie. Sweet! And now Sal too? Way to go! Help Winnie be patient with the new little horses out there."

I couldn't believe it. It was like Lizzy had read my New Year's resolutions.

"And look out for my friend Geri. Let her

know I'm here if she needs me. I'm not sure she knows how to handle this thing with Nate."

Lizzy was quiet for a whole minute, and I strained to pick up what she and God were talking privately about. Then she said, "You're right! *There is a friend who sticks closer than a brother.* Proverbs 18:24, right? Thanks for being my best friend. Night."

I started to say "Night" back, but I knew she'd said it to God.

In seconds Lizzy was making her little snoring noises. Even though the conversation had been Lizzy's and God's, I felt better.

My alarm went off a little before five. I dressed in the dark, shivering as I pulled on cold jeans and the first sweatshirt I could grab. I glanced out of the window and was amazed at how many stars shone over the pasture. I could see the big oak tree just beyond the paddock. And through the *V* of the tree, I saw the same star Catman had shown me. Polaris, the North Star.

I'd have to remember to tell Catman his star was in the exact same spot he left it.

Dad was already hunkered over the tea-kettle, pouring steaming water into his instant coffee.

"You're up early, Dad."

"Ow!" He dropped the kettle back onto the burner and shook his hand.

I ran over to him. "Sorry if I scared you."

He ran cold water on his finger, and I wiped up the spill. Then we sat down to chocolate donuts sprinkled with peppermints. Lizzy had left them out for us.

"Up all night?" I asked.

Dad touched the puffy bags under his eyes. "Well, I wouldn't have had to be up all night if *certain people* kept their promises about helping *certain other* people with their inventions."

I admit I'm not the fastest horse on the track, but I knew he was talking about Madeline. Part of me felt bad for both of them. When Dad's in the middle of working out an invention, he forgets everything else too. And Madeline *was* coming this morning to help him.

I got up and warmed a bottle of goat's milk. I needed to get Friendly to nurse from Annie. But they'd both have to calm down quite a bit before that was going to happen.

"I'm off to do barn chores, Dad. Sal's coming at 11. I'll stop by Pat's first. Need anything?"

"Uh-huh." Dad was picking at the peppermint pieces on his donut while he frowned into outer space.

I knew he was off in Inventorland. I kissed the top of his head and left. I don't think he even noticed.

The best thing about every day is the first time I see Nickers. She was lying next to the foal, her head arched over the filly's back. As soon as she heard me, she nickered and got to her feet.

That's when I saw Catman Coolidge. He was lying in the straw on the other side of the foal in the exact same position. Flat on their sides, arms crossed, long legs stretched out.

"It's groovy down here, man," he said. "Far-out, pint-sized horse view."

I couldn't believe Friendly was letting Catman that close.

He started to sit up. The filly lifted her head.

"Stay down there, Catman," I whispered.

He lay back down, and so did the foal. Nickers lowered her head to nuzzle Friendly.

"Perfect!" I whispered, easing in beside

Catman. "I need Friendly's head in my lap. But you have to keep her from pulling up. Then I'll give her a real imprinting session. Got it?"

"Negative," he said.

"Catman, you have to help! Half hour tops, okay?"

"No can do, man. Overdue at my pad. Bart-and-Claire duty."

Catman calls his parents by their first names when they're not around. "They'll understand, Catman."

He shook his head. "No time. Promised I'd help them fill out expiring contest entries."

Catman claims his dad makes more money winning contests than selling cars. But they have to enter a zillion contests a year. "I'll help!" I placed his hand on the filly's withers. She didn't budge. "So it will only take us half as long. Please, Catman?"

"Bart will freak. But I'm down with it."

We'd have to hurry, but it was too good an opportunity to pass up.

I willed my hand to move at the speed of a snail. My fingertips touched the foal's neck. She twitched, but that was all. I inched my hand up her neck, then slid my other hand under her head. With one sweep I lifted the filly's head and scooted under her so her head lay in my lap. "You'll like this once we get going, Friendly."

"Friendly?" Catman repeated. "Bad handle."

I was used to Catman's 60s language, so I knew *handle* meant *name*. I also knew he was right. "It's not her real name. I'm waiting for Mason to name her."

A picture jumped to my mind: Mason staring at the foal, the foal staring back, their eyes white with fear and distrust. Great. My photographic memory had snapped a picture of that.

Then, as if a slide show had kicked in, my mind shot me more photos, all of them of Gracie. Friendly was her baby. I owed it to that mare to give her foal a good life. Gracie had died with her head in my lap, just like this.

Catman peered over at me, his sharp, blue eyes cutting through the tiny, round lenses of his glasses. "It's cool, Winnie." That's all he said, but it was enough.

"We'll start with her head," I explained. It helped me to talk it through. And I knew it was a good idea to get the foal used to human voices.

I stroked the blaze on her forehead. Then I

touched her jaw and under her chin. When I got near her muzzle, she tossed her head to keep me away from her nose and mouth.

"When she fusses, I have to keep repeating the same strokes," I explained. "A hundred times or more. She needs to know I'll never give up on her."

When Friendly finally stopped fussing, her eyelids drooped.

"She digs it!" Catman whispered. He scooped up Nelson as the black-and-white kitty headed my way. The flat-faced Churchill, orange tabby Moggie, and Rice were already on his lap.

When I was sure the foal wasn't resisting my touch on her head, I moved to her ears. I started with the left ear, rubbing it, then massaging it. "This will make it easier to bridle her when it's time."

I stuck my finger inside her ear and wiggled it. She shook her head like it tickled, but I kept at it. "Once she gets used to people messing with her ears, she won't mind if somebody clips her ears later on. She'll remember. It's all a matter of trust, Catman."

It didn't take long for her to get used to

having her ears scratched. But I kept it up long after she stopped ear-flicking.

I moved on to the nostrils. Then the lips.

She definitely didn't like me messing with her mouth. Her lips twitched. She squirmed and lifted her head.

Amigo suddenly let out a mournful whinny.

Nickers answered it.

Annie Goat joined in.

I started in again, only I couldn't remember what I was supposed to do after the lips. There's a right order for imprinting. What if I got it wrong? I probably *was* doing it wrong. The filly was squirming more than ever.

We'd been at it a half hour, maybe way over. I'd promised to help Catman. Then I had to get to Pat's. Who knew how many e-mails had piled up for me on the Pet Help Line? Then I'd have to rush back to the barn before 11. I didn't want to miss Sal in case she came early. And Amigo. Sal and I would have to put in a couple of hours with Amigo.

"Chill, Winnie," Catman said, using both hands to hold down the filly.

Friendly twisted her neck, trying to see Nickers. The filly was picking up my nerves.

I couldn't do this. "You can let her up now, Catman. I think we need a break." But I knew it wasn't good to stop now, to give up on her.

The second Catman took his hand from her shoulder, the filly bounced up and trotted straight to Nickers to be rescued.

Nickers the Horse Gentler.

$\mathcal{C}$atman and I speed-walked through the
pasture and across the field, kicking through
ankle-deep snow. I was glad Catman had opted
out of his usual sandals in favor of moccasins.
His striped bell-bottom jeans had snow-covered
fringe on the sides that swung as he walked.
Turquoise beads peeked through his army
jacket.

"Did you get the beads for Christmas?"
I asked.

He shook his head.

"So what *did* you get?"

"Beatles," he answered. "Eight-tracks."

I'd listened to the Coolidges' eight-tracks
before. They're weird, box-shaped things that
people used before CDs got invented.

Cats swarmed between us, more of them falling in as we got nearer to Coolidge Castle. That's how I'd come to think of Catman's home. The first time I saw it, though, I thought it was a haunted house.

Rice, the big white cat, leaped into Catman's arms. He stuck the cat inside his jacket.

Long gray clouds widened in the sky, as if they were being inflated.

"Hey, Catman," I said, remembering the stars earlier. "Guess what. This morning that star of yours, the North Star, Polaris, was in the exact same spot as last night."

"Always is. Always will be."

I didn't know much about astronomy. But I did know that every time I tried to find the Big Dipper or Orion, they were in different places. "I thought stars moved around."

"Not this one."

Who knew?

Winter was definitely the best season for Coolidge Castle. The two boarded-up windows were covered with ice, and the gabled roof wore a white coating that took some of the spookiness out of the three-story rambling house.

I always check the front lawn before going

inside. Mr. Coolidge is big on lawn ornaments, and you never know what will turn up. He'd outdone himself for Christmas, filling the whole front yard with Santas—Santa mice, Santa bears, Santa dwarfs (left over from Snow White's crew).

But something new had been added. The biggest Santa Claus had been transformed into an old man, dressed in rags and holding a scythe. Next to him, one of the elves wore nothing but a diaper.

"Let me guess," I said. "Old Year, New Year?"

Catman just grinned.

We found Catman's parents at the dining-room table—a long, heavy piece of furniture with big claw feet. You could barely see the tabletop under the stacks of paper.

Coolidge Castle makes me feel like I've stepped inside a time machine and shot backward 100 years. Thick red-velvet curtains shut out the world. A giant spiral staircase leads to more rooms than I can count. You walk on Persian rugs and thick red carpet and stare up at sky-high ceilings.

"Calvin!" cried his mother. "Is that you?"

We couldn't see her over the paper piles, but nobody except Claire Coolidge would call Catman "Calvin."

She kept talking. "Do you know what will happen if we fail to fill out all of these expiring contest entries? What will *not* happen, I should say. We may miss winning a brand-new, precision-made tricycle! Or a year's supply of dog food. Or a two-year supply of Crispy Rice Flakes!"

I knew nobody in the house rode a tricycle. A couple dozen cats were creeping from every room, but no dogs. And I didn't know where they'd put one more box of cereal. Their cupboards were full of cereal boxes, each one with a rectangle cut out from the back for last month's cereal contest.

"Where do we start?" I asked.

Chair legs scraped the floor. Then the head and shoulders of Mrs. Claire Coolidge popped up over the paper pile. Her head was covered with giant juice cans that had been transformed into hair curlers. She wore a fuzzy green bathrobe that matched the green netting over her juice-can curlers.

"Is that Winnie?" She brushed aside enough entry forms to see better. "It's *really* you!" She got up and charged around the table toward me. "Winnie, Winnie, *Winnie!*"

Maybe one of the reasons I like coming to

Coolidge Castle so much is that Catman's mother always acts like she hasn't seen me for years and is really thrilled I came over.

She hugged me hard. Then she reached up and whisked off my stocking cap. "There! Let's have a look at that gorgeous hair!"

Claire Coolidge is the only one, to my knowledge, who thinks *I* have gorgeous hair. Gorgeous hair is Lizzy's department. Mine is wild as a Mustang and ornery as a Shetland.

"For a minute, I thought you'd cut this lovely hair." She tried to run her fingers through it but didn't get far. Too many tangles.

It was funny because I *had* been thinking about chopping off my hair.

As if she were reading my mind she said, "Winifred Willis, if you ever cut your hair, I will sell my salon and follow you around, scolding, until every inch of hair grows back."

Note to self: Don't cut your hair.

I glanced down at her fuzzy green slippers, topped on each toe by a stuffed Tweety Bird head. No doubt a gift from her husband.

"*Sa-a-ay!* How are you, young Winnie?" Bart Coolidge gave me his best firm, used-car-salesman handshake. Even though it was only six in the morning, he was wearing a gray-striped suit, with his Tweety Bird necktie loosened around the neck of his canary-yellow shirt.

"I'm fine, Mr. Coolidge. I'm the one who made Catman late. But I'm going to help him make up for lost time."

"That's fine then!" he boomed. *"Sa-a-ay!"*

I felt a joke coming on. Even though Mr. Coolidge is a natural used-car salesman, he must have dreamed of being a comedian. He has more jokes than a Pinto has spots.

"Knock-knock!"

I was already starting to laugh. His jokes are so corny that I can't help it. "Who's there?" I knew my part by now.

"Wire!" he shouted.

"Wire who?"

"Why're you here and not out at Smart Bart's Used Cars taking advantage of our great, end-of-year bargains?"

We both laughed until our eyes watered.

Mrs. Coolidge brought out tomatoes, the Coolidge family's favorite snack. We each took one and started in on it.

Catman and I dug into the pile of entry blanks. Mrs. Coolidge insisted that I put in my own name, and whatever I won, I got to keep.

I filled out contest forms to win a toaster oven, a case of Spaghetti Ws, a month's supply of Alphabet Rice, the world's largest garden hose, a year's worth of free movies for cable TV, which we don't have. But Catman handed me one entry I would have loved to win. A week at a dude ranch in Colorado. The fine print said the odds were 1,300,000 to 1.

"Maybe you'll follow in your father's lucky footsteps," Mrs. Coolidge said, passing her husband another stack of envelopes. "Didn't he win an invention contest?"

"With the back bike," I said.

"I have to get one of those bikes!" Mrs. Coolidge declared.

"You know," I said, reading the entries more closely, "these just have to be *postmarked* by January 1. We don't really *have* to finish them today." I was starting to worry about the time. I knew I hadn't put in my fair share yet, but I was anxious to get to the help line.

"But we're leaving at noon!" Mr. Coolidge announced.

"Where are you going?" I asked.

"Didn't Calvin tell you?" Mrs. Coolidge frowned at her son, who kept filling out entries at record speed.

"I can't believe you didn't tell your little friend about our prize!" Mrs. Coolidge scolded.

"What did you win?" I asked.

Mrs. Coolidge smiled so wide that I saw silver fillings on her back teeth. "Bart and I won an all-expenses-paid vacation to 15 international cities!"

"Wow! That's so great! What a trip!" I couldn't even imagine visiting *one* foreign city. I turned to Catman. "Catman, do you get to go?" I thought that for a trip like that, the principal wouldn't even count him absent.

Catman shook his head. "Barkers'."

Mrs. Coolidge explained. "I'm afraid we only won *two* vacations. Calvin will stay with Eddy Barker."

"It's a *romantic*, all-expenses-paid vacation, don't forget!" Mr. Coolidge chimed in. He leaned over and kissed his wife on top of her head, but it ended up being a kiss on a big green curler.

"So where are you going?" I asked, thinking I'd choose somewhere in Italy or Spain.

Mrs. Coolidge counted on her fingers as she spoke. I noticed that she wore eight rings, skipping only the pinkie and thumb of her left hand.

"1. Paris
2. Vienna
3. Warsaw
4. Nineveh
5. Bethlehem
6. Calcutta
7. Berlin
8. Athens
9. Antwerp
10. Belfast
11. El Dorado
12. London
13. Dresden
14. Moscow
15. Utopia"

"I-I can't believe you get to go to all those cities!" I didn't know where Utopia was, but I recognized most of the others. "Are they all safe?" I'd heard about fighting in Belfast. And Moscow had always sounded kind of scary to me.

"Oh my, yes!" Mrs. Coolidge assured me. "I plan to visit beauty shops in every city too.

As we all know, there is no safer place on earth than a beauty salon."

I, for one, hadn't known that. But Mrs. Coolidge runs a hair salon, so she ought to know.

"Hard job narrowing down possible cities," said Mr. Coolidge, licking an envelope. "I really wanted to see Lebanon, Vera Cruz, Sodom, and Poznan. But I gave in gladly to the lovely Mrs. Coolidge."

"That's not exactly how I remember it, Mr. Coolidge," his wife countered. "As I recall, *I* really wanted to visit Palermo, Jerusalem, Amsterdam, Congo, Canaan, and Cuba. And *I* was the one who gave in to the charming *Mr.* Coolidge."

Mr. Coolidge got up from his chair so fast that it tipped over. He ran to his wife and threw his arms around her. "My darling!" He swung her to the side, like ballroom dancers dipping, and kissed her. "Let's never fight again."

"No, never!" she answered.

That was a fight?

Note to self: Get Dad and Madeline in the same room as Mr. and Mrs. Coolidge, then bring up the golf buddy.

This was definitely not a fight.

"So how long will you be gone?" I asked when they were both upright again.

"Four days," Mrs. Coolidge said.

*F*our days? You mean four *weeks?*" I couldn't
see how they'd squeeze all those cities into four
weeks. But I didn't think they'd leave Catman
for four *months.*

"Four days," Mr. Coolidge said, picking up his
toppled chair. "We don't stay in all the cities.
Some we dine in. Others we drive through."

"And only check out their beauty salons,"
Mrs. Coolidge added.

"And their used-car lots," Mr. Coolidge
continued.

I wasn't getting this at all. "But how can you?
Four *days?* You'll barely get to the first city and
have to fly to another, then another. . . ."

Mr. Coolidge frowned at me as if I'd said a
dirty word. *"Fly?* Our stops aren't that far apart,
Winnie."

I'd heard people say Americans *think* European countries are all bunched together like the state of Iowa, but we're wrong. They *are* far apart once you try to travel from one to the other.

"Besides," bellowed Mr. Coolidge, "would Smart Bart be seen in an airplane?" The way he pronounced it, it sounded like *arrowplane*.

Now I really wasn't getting it. They *had* to fly to Europe. I looked to Catman for help.

Even though his mouth was a straight line, his blue eyes were laughing at me. "European cities . . . in Ohio."

"Your parents won a trip to Ohio? Their own state?"

"We've agreed to only speak the appropriate language in each bed-and-breakfast," Mrs. Coolidge went on. "We won't be talking much through Moscow and Warsaw."

"Who needs words, my little Cadillac?" Mr. Coolidge cooed.

When the grandfather clock struck nine, I started worrying about the help line and getting done in time to get back for Sal and Amigo.

Catman must have read my mind. "Gotta split."

His parents thanked us for helping. I told them to have a great vacation, but I already knew they would.

The light was on and the dogs were up and barking when we walked into Pat's Pets.

Pat Haven, the owner, is kind of a permanent sub for my seventh-grade life science class. She's a good teacher and a great friend.

"Hey, Winnie. Catman," Pat said, coming over to us. "How's that filly doing?"

"She's okay. Doesn't like me much, though. I'm trying to imprint her, but it's tough."

Pat shook her head like this was terrible news. Usually she's one of the bounciest people I know. But today even her brown curls weren't springy. Dressed in a yoked shirt and blue jeans, she looked like a cowgirl who'd just lost the rodeo.

"You okay, Pat?" I asked.

"That twit's got me wound tighter than a rattlesnake. No offense." Pat always apologizes

87

to the animals she uses in her expressions. This apology was aimed in the general direction of the boa constrictor. "Don't know what I'm supposed to do with that little twit."

I couldn't believe it. Pat Haven had just called someone a *twit*. Twice! It wasn't like her. Even at middle school, which is populated by a high percentage of twits, I've never heard her say anything bad about anybody.

"Who, Pat?" I asked.

"Dollface," she answered.

I should have known. "You mean that big goldfish?"

Pat nodded.

"Why is she a twit?" I asked, wondering how much trouble a goldfish could be.

"She's pregnant!" Pat laughed. "That's what a *twit* is—a pregnant goldfish." She stopped laughing as suddenly as if somebody had shut her off. "She's not looking so good, if you ask me."

"I don't know much about fish, Pat," I confessed.

"Cats eat them," Catman said, shrugging.

"Hey, guys! Almost done!" Barker shouted from the other side of the store, where Pat has a computer just for the Pet Help Line.

Catman and I made our way past the iguana cage over to Barker. Zorro was sitting on Barker's lap, not even trying to scramble off. His imprinting must have been going a whole lot better than Friendly's.

"I only had one message today," Barker said, tucking Zorro like a football under one arm before he got up. Barker motioned for one of us to take the computer. "Three e-mails for you, Catman. Winnie, you've got a dozen."

I let Catman go first so he could get home before his parents left on their tour. And, anyway, I love seeing what Catman writes.

Before he checked his own e-mail, Catman hit keys so fast I couldn't tell what he'd done. But there was Barker's question-and-answer on the screen. I guess Catman liked reading Barker's e-mails as much as I enjoyed Catman's. I wondered if anybody enjoyed mine.

I moved around so I could read too:

Dear Barker,

Help! I'm worried about Albert, my dog. He's only 9 months old, and I think he's got leprosy! Small black spots popped out on his lower lips and face.

And his chin has crusty, yucky spots.
What should I do?
—Albert the First

Dear Albert,
   Don't worry. Those black spots . . .
they're zits! You heard me. Dog
pimples. Lots of puppies get them.
Dogs too.
   Wash Albert's face twice a day. Keep
his food dish clean. Stay away from
plastic bowls because they hold the oil
and get it on your puppy's chin. Stick
with aluminum or glass or pottery or
even china.
—Barker

Catman switched to his e-mails and got right
to it, typing at Quarter Horse speed, using only
his thumbs and pinkies.

Dear Catman,
   I think our family cat hates me. The
minute I get close to her, she rolls on
her back and sticks her claws up in the
air. It's probably my fault. When I was a

little kid, I was scared of cats. I'm not now, but maybe our cat remembers and won't give me another chance.
—Catman Wanna-be

Hey, Cat!

Never fear! That ol' cat digs you, man! Cats don't roll over for any ol' jive turkey! Belly up means, "I trust you totally, Daddy-O!" And don't sweat the past cat fear. That little fighting dude named Napoleon had a bad case of ailurophobia (fear of cats) too. Only he never got rid of it.

Be cool, Cat!
—The Catman

Dear Catman,

I am an old man who loves his cats. All three of my cats have been getting sick off and on all winter. The vet says they're fine. But whenever the cats go outside, they come back in and groan with stomachaches an hour later. Then they're fine again. I keep my walks shoveled and salted just so the cats

won't have to walk in the cold snow.
Any ideas for me?
—Old-Timer

Dear Old-Timer,
   Might be the salt on your walks, man!
That stuff gets soaked in through cats'
paws. Plus cats lick it off their little
doggies (paws). Lose the salt. Sounds
like you four cats are a groovy four-
some!
—The Catman

When it was my turn, I scrolled through
e-mails and pulled out the easy ones. Seven of
the questions had to do with problem horses
who had been cooped up in stalls all winter.
They cribbed or chewed on their stalls. They
pawed and spooked at everything.

The horses needed to get outside more.
Anybody would go crazy from boredom just
standing in a box stall night and day. I told them
to turn out their horses as often as they could.
And I suggested ways they could make the stall
more fun with hay nets and toys.

It was the first time I'd ever cut and pasted
answers on the help line, copying the same

answer for all seven e-mails. I felt bad and promised myself I'd never do it again. But I only had an hour, so I had to.

I worked my way through the rest of the e-mails. One horse resented the new horse in the barn. One owner needed advice on cleaning out the frog, the V-shaped underneath part of the hoof. One girl needed me to tell her that her horse's natural winter coat would have been a better protector than the stall blanket she'd left on all winter.

The longest answer went to Confused in Colorado:

> Dear Winnie the Horse Gentler,
>
> Molly is the best Morgan in the whole world. Every day for the four months I've owned her, I brushed her from head to hoof. I thought she loved it. But a week ago she started acting weird. Whenever I'd get to her hindquarters, she'd lift her back leg, like she was going to kick me! It's SO not like her! But now she does it every time I get near her rump or try to walk around her. Help!
>
> —Confused in Colorado

Dear Confused,

You're smart to pay attention to your horse when she lifts her hind leg like that. With lots of horses, it's their way of warning you they'll kick. But I don't think that's what Molly's saying to you. You said she loves the brushing, right? Well, I think she's saying, "All right! Here she comes. She's going to scratch and massage my leg again. I can hardly wait!"

The hindquarters are hard for a horse to reach, especially in a stall. She's ready for you to help her out. Good broodmares lift that hind leg when their foals get near. They're ready to nurse their babies.

Be careful until you're sure this is what Molly's saying to you. It's possible she has a sore area or is ticklish. But I'll bet if you go ahead and brush her (staying to her side, just in case), she'll sigh a big thank you.

—Winnie the Horse Gentler

Pat ambled over just as I finished the last e-mail. All of my answers had been shorter than

I would have liked. But I'd finished in time to get back to the barn and groom Amigo before Sal got there.

"Everything hunky-dory?" Pat asked.

"All done," I answered. "Except there are two bird questions I couldn't answer. Want me to leave them until Hawk gets back?"

"Hot dog! No offense." She waved at the collie pup in the nearest cage. "Hawk! Why didn't I think of her before? That girl knows a lot about fish! She might be able to help me with the twit."

Hawk knows everything about birds, but Pat was right. Hawk knows her fish too.

"Do you know how to reach her? Florida, right?" Pat queried.

"I've got her number at home. I guess I could—"

"Terrific! Call home. Then we'll give that little lady a call." Pat looked more like herself again.

I wanted to go home and start in on Amigo, but I couldn't make Pat wait any longer. I picked up the phone.

"I hear tell you're housing a Mini for a spell," Pat said as I dialed my number.

"Yeah. He's beautiful. But he doesn't trust me yet," I admitted.

The phone rang once.

"Well, I suppose it's not that all-fired impor-tant, what with him leaving so soon and all."

My insides went cold. "What do you mean, Pat?"

"I ran in to Mrs. Cracker last night. Over at A-Mart. Checkout line. I know, I know. I wasn't going to shop at the Spidell empire, but I needed those little bitty carrots already chopped and in the bag for—"

"Pat, what did she say about Amigo?"

"She was just saying how Sal and that Mini didn't take to each other."

Someone answered the phone. Dad. "Hello?"

I hung up. "And? What else did Mrs. Cracker say?"

Finally Pat looked at me. Her smile faded. "I'm sorry, Winnie. I didn't think I was telling you anything you didn't already know. Mrs. Cracker said she's tying a big *RETURN TO SENDER* sign around that Mini's neck and ship-ping him back on the first boat to Argentina."

I stood there, clutching the disconnected phone. *Back to Argentina?*

I couldn't let that happen. That poor little horse had been through enough. "I've got to go," I said, getting up.

"Winnie? What about Hawk? My twit?" Pat's worried voice brought me back.

"I'm sorry. I forgot. Give me a minute. I'll call home."

Dad answered on the first ring. "Hello?"

"Hi, Dad. It's me."

"Oh. Winnie." He sounded like I was the last person he wanted to speak to.

"Um . . . I need to get Hawk's number in Florida. It's on the—"

"I'll get Lizzy." The phone clunked.

Then it clunked again. "Winnie?"

"Hi, Lizzy. What's wrong with Dad? Golf-buddy problems?"

"More like invention-buddy problems. Madeline said she'd be here a couple of hours ago."

In the background I heard Dad shout, "Tell her to get off the phone! Madeline may be trying to call again."

"The phone rang, and somebody hung up on Dad," Lizzy explained. "Dad thinks it was Madeline."

"That was me. Sorry."

"Poor Dad." Lizzy sighed through the phone line. "Have to admit . . . I thought it might be Geri."

"You *still* haven't heard from her?" I felt myself getting mad at Geri all over again.

"No. I kind of thought she'd show up this morning."

Pat paced by, reminding me why I'd called home. Lizzy gave me Hawk's number, and I made her promise to hold on to Sal if she showed up before I got there.

Pat dialed Florida, then handed the phone back to me.

"She might not even be there," I said while the phone rang. "She's been showing Towaco in Florida horse shows, so—"

"Hello?" It was Hawk's dad.

"Uh . . ."

"Hello?" he said louder. "Who is this?"

"It's me, Mr. Hawkins. Winnie Willis. Can I talk to Hawk? Please?" My telephone voice is even worse than my regular voice. I hate it.

Hawk got on and started right in about her New Year's Eve party. I would have loved to listen to how great it was going to be, but Pat was waiting.

I explained about the help line e-mails, then read them to Hawk over the phone.

The first one was from a kid whose big brother kept telling him that he had too many birds. Big Brother said it was bad for the birds and bad for Little Brother.

"Tell the bird owner there is no such thing as too many birds. And that he'd be better off with loads of feathered friends," Hawk said. "Tell him that Thomas Alva Edison had over 5,000 birds, and he was our greatest inventor."

I wrote down everything in longhand.

The other question was from someone named Paula, who was worried about her parrot. Chiquita had started doing crazy things, like standing in her water dish and doing weird dances and making odd noises.

Hawk said, "That poor parrot is bored! Boredom can lead to madness in parrots. Birds need affection and interaction. If they spend too much time alone in a cage, they can lose their minds. There are even mental institutions for parrots. Tell her she should get Chiquita a friend."

"Thanks, Hawk."

There was a pause. Then Hawk asked, "Winnie, is anything wrong?"

I wanted to shout into the receiver, *"Yes! Everything's wrong! I can't get close to Friendly Foal. Sal and her grandmother want to send Amigo back to Argentina. And what I really need is for you to leave the fun and sun and get back here and help me!"*

But I couldn't say that.

"I'm okay, Hawk. Here. Let me pass you to Pat. She wants to ask you about her twit."

Pat took the phone. "Thanks, Winnie. You get on home. I'll type the bird e-mails."

As I left the shop I heard Pat exclaim, "That's all? And that twit will be as happy as a clam? No offense."

As soon as I got outside, the worries inside me started swirling around and bumping into each other, piling up like snowflakes in a blizzard. I breathed in air so cold it froze my nose hairs.

Then without even thinking about it, I shot up a prayer: *God, don't let them send that little horse to Argentina! Please! Amigo needs a friend. Let me be it. Okay? Help me be a faithful friend to that horse.*

It surprised me that I'd prayed like that. On-the-spot prayer was something Lizzy might do. Or Mom. Until the last couple of months, God and I had barely been on speaking terms. But little by little I'd figured out that God wasn't going to give up on me. Mom's dying wasn't God's fault, or even my fault. And God cared about me too much to let me get away with giving him the silent treatment.

I could feel my stomach stop swirling. I would be the best friend Amigo and Friendly ever had. No matter how *they* acted. Even if they didn't think of me as a friend, that's what I'd be.

Maybe that's the way it had been with God and me. I'd sure done everything *I* could to wrestle further away from him after Mom died. But he'd waited patiently for me.

I'd wait patiently for the horses. I wouldn't give up on *them*.

I was halfway home and feeling a lot better, in spite of the icy wind numbing my face, when who should I see coming up Claremont but Geri and Nathan.

"Hi, Winnie!" Nathan waved and sprinted toward me. He was wearing a gray coat and gray mittens, so ordinary that his sister wouldn't have been caught dead in them.

Geri lagged back and seemed to be studying a snowdrift.

Nathan is about Lizzy's height, maybe two inches taller than me. He doesn't look much like Sal. She's slim as a racehorse. Nathan's more like a small Clydesdale. Sal used to say her brother lived for the days Lizzy brought in treats to their class. Maybe he'd eaten a few too many lizard cookies.

"Is Lizzy with you?" Nathan asked, peering around me.

I shook my head.

He seemed disappointed. "Tell her hi for me when you see her." The way he said it wasn't like he was lovesick or anything, not like Geri must have been for him. My guess was that Nate liked Lizzy for a friend. Everybody does.

I stared at Geri. She finally met my gaze, then stared down again.

"That's some horse Gram Cracker gave my sister, huh?" Nathan said.

"Look, Nathan. You guys *can't* send Amigo back to Argentina. I need time to work with him. He's a good horse. He'll make a great pet." For all I knew, Nathan felt just like Sal did about horses. But it was worth a shot.

"I wish Gram Cracker had given that little horse to *me*," Nathan said.

I was trying not to like this kid, but he was making it tough. "So talk to them, Nathan. Make them give me a chance with Amigo. Okay?"

"Okay," he promised. "But nobody ever listens to me."

"I have to get to the barn. Sal's coming over. Come by sometime, *Nathan*," I said, leaving out Geri on purpose.

Geri looked up. "Is Lizzy mad?"

Nathan frowned back at her like he had no

idea what she meant. "Lizzy? She's never mad at anybody."

"Why don't you call her and ask her, Geri?" I said.

I ran the rest of the way home and got there exactly two minutes after 11. First I checked the barn. Sal wasn't there.

Then I ran inside. "Lizzy! Is Sal here?"

Lizzy met me in the hall. Larry the Lizard was curled up on her shoulder. "No." Then she added, "Neither is Madeline."

I thought about telling Lizzy about seeing Nathan and Geri, but I didn't want to hurt her feelings. My sister has been the most popular girl in every class she's been in, including all the schools in the *I* states—Illinois, Indiana, and Iowa—where we didn't stay long. She's not popular in the same way Summer Spidell is. Most girls in middle school want to be like Summer. But I'm not sure how many of them actually *like* her. Lizzy, on the other hand, everybody likes.

Still, even though there were a couple dozen

girls Lizzy could have invited over, it had to hurt that her *best* friend had tossed her aside for a boy.

I raced back to the barn. The wind blew snow from the trees and moved white swirls of it from the ground, making it look like a snowstorm. Catman calls it a "recycled blizzard."

I said hi to Nickers and Friendly and eased into Amigo's stall.

The little Falabella shuffled deeper into the corner.

I kept my distance and watched him. Mom taught me that horses need their space. She had pretended there was a large circle around every horse, space that belonged to him. "Wait for the horse to let you in," she'd said. "Inviting us in is a leap of faith."

Staying out of Amigo's space, I tried to imagine what he was feeling. I didn't know if he'd traveled from Argentina by boat or by plane. I just knew he'd come a long way without any friends. And so far he hadn't found any here.

"I'm here when you're ready, Amigo," I said, wishing I'd paid attention in Iowa when we had six weeks of Spanish. But I knew Amigo wouldn't care what language I spoke. He wouldn't even care that my voice sounds like I have laryngitis.

Amigo's head drooped lower.

"You know, Amigo, Sal's not such a bad person once you get to know her. Not that *I* really know her. She has a lot of friends in middle school. You wouldn't like it there. It's hard to break into those herds. They stampede through the halls, and any new-comer who tries to join a herd gets kicked out."

I watched Amigo for signs of softening. One ear twitched, and I took it as an invitation to take one step inside his circle.

"I know you've had it tough, boy. No wonder you're scared."

Both ears twitched.

I kept talking—about the foal, about Nickers, even about Lizzy and Geri.

Finally I got a clear go-ahead. Amigo craned his neck around to see me. His ears pointed toward me, then flicked side to side.

"Don't mind if I do," I said, walking slowly until I reached him. It was weird to reach *down*, instead of *up*, to pet him.

His back twitched.

I kept scratching him on the withers, where most horses love it. Amigo didn't seem to, though.

I searched for his secret spot, the part of him that yearned to be scratched. I hoped it wasn't his hind leg, like the horse in the e-mail. I didn't quite trust Amigo not to kick me yet.

Not until I moved in front of him did I find it. When I scratched a spot above his chest, he stretched out his head and begged for more.

"You like that, don't you, Amigo? See? You can trust me."

Someone clomped into the barn. I hadn't heard a car drive up, but I heard one take off— fast. Probably Gram Cracker's van.

I started to yell for Sal but thought better of it. I didn't want to scare Amigo just when he was getting used to me.

"Well, where is she?" Instead of Sal, Summer Spidell thundered down the stallway.

Just what I needed.

$\mathcal{M}$erry Christmas and Happy New Year to you too, Summer," I called in a fake, cheery voice, as I kept scratching Amigo. His brown eyes closed to half-mast.

"I'm not kidding!" she shouted, frowning into the stall at us. "Where is Sal?"

Summer was wearing a long palomino colored coat with a matching fuzzy hat and scarf. Her long blonde hair curled below her shoulders. "I'm in a hurry, Winifred."

Summer Spidell is about the only person who calls me that, and she only does it to make me mad. It works every time, but I try not to show it.

"So? Where is she?" she repeated louder, in

case *all* of Ashland hadn't heard her. "Sal told me she was coming over here."

"Well, I'm not hiding her, if that's what you're thinking."

I heard a car and hoped it was someone coming for Summer. The car stopped outside the barn, and a door slammed.

"Sal!" Summer screamed, running from the barn as if it were on fire.

I heard both of them squeal the way popular girls do when they see each other in school on Monday mornings or after a break.

"Humans," I whispered to Amigo, not letting up on his scratching. His eyes closed all the way. I wondered if he could shut out the world like Mason Edison. And which one could teach me that.

Sal and Summer kind of flowed back into the barn together, ignoring me. So what else was new? At school they're in the same popular group. So they sit together in classes, at lunch, everywhere. But Summer had been even more clingy to Sal than usual, since Hawk had been gone.

Summer and Sal kept talking so loudly that Amigo and I couldn't help overhearing.

"Grant said Brian was going to call you and

apologize. Did he?" Summer asked, like
the whole world depended on the answer.

"He called," Sal answered. "I'm still hacked
off at him for standing me up, though. That's
the third time this month. I mean, if somebody
says they'll come over or call, they should do
it."

I nearly choked, then cleared my throat to
cover it. *From Sal's mouth to Sal's ears!*

"He's just a guy," Summer observed. "So
you're all made up, though, right? The four of us
can go to Hawk's party together?"

Maybe that wouldn't be so bad. Maybe
Hawk would hang out with me more on
New Year's Eve if Sal and Summer were
with guys. I had to admit that the more I
thought about Hawk's New Year's Eve party,
the more I looked forward to it. It wouldn't just
be the first New Year's Eve party for me. It
would be the first *party*. I'd been to birthday
parties when we lived in Wyoming and to
family-and-friend stuff. But never a *real* party
like this.

"Are those new jeans?" Summer asked,
sounding as if she didn't approve.

"Nope. These are *old* jeans, with *new* fat in

them. What I don't get is how a *one*-pound box of candy can make me gain *five* pounds."

Seriously, Sal's almost as skinny as Madeline. It was hard to believe she worried about gaining weight. Summer was psycho about weight gain. Maybe it had rubbed off on Sal. I wondered if Sal liked the extra attention she was getting from Summer, or if she was as eager to get Hawk home as I was.

"I'll help you lose that extra weight," Summer offered. "What are friends for? We'll get it off before school starts. In the meantime don't wear those jeans when you're with Brian."

I thought about interrupting them before I puked, but the feeling passed.

"I can't wait to buy that gold sweater I told you about," Summer cooed. "It will look *so* great on me!"

"I thought Grant was getting it for you for Christmas," Sal said.

"He didn't get the hint. He got me a *scarf*." Summer made it sound like he'd gotten her earthworms. "My grandmother got me a scarf. Richard got me a scarf. Aunt Lisa got me a scarf. If I get one more cashmere scarf, I'm going to strangle myself with it!"

Note to self: Save up for a cashmere scarf for Summer.

I couldn't take it anymore. "Amigo and I are ready for you, Sal!"

"Yeah. In a minute, Winnie," Sal called back.

"Your horse is already calmer," I said, leaving the stall to join Summer and Sal. "I'll show you how to imprint him. I don't think he's going to be much of a problem."

"Sal!" Summer squealed. "You *promised* we could go to the mall together. I *have* to get that sweater I'm in love with! They only had two left in my size!"

"We just need about two hours, Sal," I said, hoping Summer wouldn't want to wait in the barn. "Maybe you could meet Summer there when we're done."

"I didn't know this would take so long," Sal said. She glanced at Amigo, who had gone back to stand in the corner of the stall. "Are you sure you need me, Winnie?"

Summer took Sal's arm. "You don't need her, do you, Winnie?"

"Her horse needs her!" I answered, fighting the urge to grab Sal's other arm and have a tug-of-war with Summer. *I* would have won.

Outside a horn honked and wheels spun on ice as a black Mustang came tearing down our street.

"Richard's here," Summer announced.

Richard Spidell is Summer's brother. He's a junior in high school, and just about every girl except me thinks he's the most handsome guy in school.

"Richard?" Sal said, her hand going to the stair-step gold earrings that climbed both of her ears. Obviously Sal shared the majority opinion about Summer's brother.

"He's driving us to the mall," Summer said, making *ma-all* sound like two syllables that should be set to music.

"That's so tight!" Sal squealed.

"But your horse!" I protested, knowing Amigo and I didn't stand a chance against Richard and the *ma-all*.

Sal shrugged and let herself be led away by Summer. "Don't worry about the midget, Winnie!" she called back. "Gram says we're probably sending it back anyway."

"No!" I shouted. "Sal, come back tomorrow! After church! You'll see how sweet Amigo is!"

"Okay!" she hollered back.

"I mean it, Sal!"

I trudged from the barn to the house. The sun had given up, turning the outside world dark gray.

The second I opened the front door, I was struck with the aroma of fresh-baked cookies. "Lizzy, what did you bake?" I shouted, pulling off my boots. It was pretty amazing how Lizzy's kitchen concoctions could sweep in and push out at least some of the rottenness left by Summer.

Lizzy called out from the kitchen, "I didn't bake anything. Catman did it!"

I hurried to the kitchen to find Catman in Dad's white barbeque apron. Striped bell-bottoms and a tie-dyed T-shirt showed through. Lizzy's flowered oven mittens covered his hands as he pulled a sheet of cookies from the oven. He set it on top of the stove and looked like he'd just won a horse show.

"Outta sight!" Catman exclaimed, staring at

the cookie lumps that might have been cat-shaped.

"And he did them all by himself!" Lizzy winked at me.

I took a closer look. Every cookie had M&M's forming the number 4 in blue or brown. "They look great, Catman. But how come they all say *four*?"

"I dig the number 4," he answered, as if I were the crazy one for asking.

I plopped at the kitchen table and let Lizzy and Catman wait on me. The oven heat felt great, and my fingers tingled as they thawed out. I took a sip of what looked like orange juice but tasted like lemon and cranberry.

Dad strode up the hall, past the kitchen, and straight to the phone. He frowned at it, huffed, then started to go out.

"How's it going, Dad?" I asked.

Dad stopped, as if shocked to see us. "Hi, Winnie. Catman. Lizzy. Didn't see you there."

Catman had a mouthful of sticky number-4 cookie, but he grinned hello.

The phone rang.

"I got it!" Dad shouted, running for the phone. "Hello?"

There was a pause.

Then Dad shouted into the phone, "No, you may *not* speak with the lady of the house!" He slammed the receiver, then walked off, muttering to himself, "Of course, the phone isn't for me." He stuck his hands in his pockets and came out with two charcoal-covered golf balls. "Why would anyone call me? Who would care enough to call, much less come over and . . . ?" His voice trailed off down the hall.

Poor Dad. And poor Madeline, when she finally did call.

Lizzy poured Catman another glass of lemon-cranberry juice and changed the subject. "Everything tastes better in shapes, don't you think?"

After two more cookies, Catman stood to go. "See you cats on the flip side."

After Catman left, I helped Lizzy with dishes. Then I heated goat's milk and headed back to the barn.

Inside, a steady stream of cats was flowing toward the stalls. And from the barn came a series of squeaky, scrappy, unidentifiable squeals.

 dashed into the barn, almost tripping over
the white-haired Rice. The screeches came
together into words and echoed off the barn
walls: "And I'll be-e-e there-ere-ere. You got a
friend, baby. You got a friend, darling. Don't you
know that you got a frie-e-end!"

"Catman?" I called, following the sound of his
voice, which led right to Nickers' stall.

I stopped. There was Catman, holding Annie
Goat's halter. The goat was standing perfectly
still on a hay bale. And beneath her, Friendly
Foal was nursing as if she couldn't get enough.

"You did it!" I cried. "You got the foal to drink
from that ornery goat."

I slipped into the stall and hoisted myself onto
Nickers' bare back for a better view. Nickers and

I watched as the foal drank, and the Catman kept singing, working his spell on Annie Goat.

Even Amigo sneaked closer to peer into the stall.

When it looked like Friendly had had her fill, Catman let go of Annie. The goat hopped off the bale of hay and took a bite out of it. Nickers strolled over and nuzzled the foal.

It was too great a moment to let go.

"Catman, can you stay and help me imprint Friendly?"

"I'm hip," he said. I took it as a yes.

I slid off Nickers and sat beside Friendly. Catman squatted down and lifted the foal into his arms. Friendly was so full and content, she barely struggled.

I laughed. "For the rest of her life, Friendly will believe you can pick her up off the ground whenever you want to." Mom had a friend who lifted her Clydesdale foals for just that reason.

Catman stretched the foal on her side, with her head in my lap.

I went over everything we'd already covered. Friendly didn't mind when I touched her neck, head, mouth, or ears. Then I moved down her neck to her mane, then her shoulders, then her rib cage. Getting her to relax when I stroked her chest was the toughest.

"If we get her used to having her chest rubbed," I explained, "she won't mind when people fasten the girth and saddle her up."

Finally I shifted around so I could stroke the foal's upper legs. I must have done it over 100 times before she stopped jerking her front legs away. Her hind legs were even tougher. But we kept at it, not giving up on her.

Sometime during the session Catman started singing softly: "'Wild Thing. You make my heart sing.'"

I grinned up at him. People used to call Nickers Wild Thing. That was before I had her. A picture flashed into my mind—a good one this time. The amazing white Arabian the first time I saw her, racing up the lane toward Lizzy and me. *That's* a picture I don't mind replaying.

I flexed Friendly's elbows, then massaged her hock and stifle, moving down the hind legs again. Then I went back to her front legs to tackle hooves. When I touched her front hoof, she struck out at me.

"Cool it, little horse," Catman said, slipping it into the tune of "Wild Thing."

I didn't let up. I rubbed the bottom of the hoof, patted it, then tapped 50 taps. "So many horses throw fits when the farrier tries to trim their hooves or shoe them for the first time. None of the horses Mom raised ever did, though."

Catman had a way of listening, even when he was singing.

Finally Friendly stayed relaxed, even when I tapped the bottom of her hooves.

"Now we need to roll her over and work her right side. Horses have two sides of the brain and fewer connections, like nerve fibers and stuff," I explained. "So it's almost like two brains. You have to train skills on both sides of a horse. Mom said people who don't know that get really frustrated because they think the horse is used to something, like laundry flapping on a line when they're riding up a road. Then they turn around and come back, and the horse acts like he's never seen laundry before."

Catman lifted the foal and rolled her over so Friendly was partway on both of us.

"This side could be tougher. The left side of the brain controls thinking and reasoning. The right side is all instinct, with survival reactions, like flight. It's the side of the brain that tells the horse to get out of there when there's trouble."

Nickers moved in closer. She leaned down and licked Friendly's neck and jaw. Instantly the foal quit struggling.

I started over, taking my time, enjoying every second, feeling myself relax with Friendly.

I'd just moved to the nostrils and lips when I heard a van door slam. The last thing we needed was to be interrupted.

"Catman, tell whoever it is to go away!"

He started to get up, but the foal didn't like that.

"No. Don't get up!" I cried.

Madeline and Mason breezed into the barn. Madeline was singing, "'Let it snow! Let it snow! Let it snow!'" in some key that hadn't been invented yet.

The foal squirmed, and I couldn't blame her.

"Hi!" I whispered, hoping they'd get the hint.

Madeline stopped singing. "Here we are! Better late than never!" But her voice always sounds like a cartoon jingle. It was all I could do to hold on to the foal.

Mason tiptoed inside the stall and stared at the foal. He looked so much like a little angel that it hurt when I remembered how I'd yelled at him.

"Is she sick?" Mason asked.

"No!" But no wonder he thought that, with the foal lying on my lap, like Gracie had. I wondered if even Madeline knew how smart that kid was. "She's great, Mason. I'm getting her used to people so she'll be a good friend for you."

"Come on over, little man!" Catman called.

Mason tiptoed behind us and slid into Catman's lap.

Madeline moved closer and watched, while I helped Mason stroke the foal's head and neck. Friendly was so good. Mason grinned until his dimple showed.

"I need to go in and help Jack," Madeline said. "Mason, do you want to come with me or stay here?"

"Stay!" Mason answered.

"Then I'll leave you kids to your fun."

She really *was* in a good mood. *Her* invention must have been going great.

I thought about Dad and how the last time I'd seen him he'd yelled at a telemarketer, something I'd never seen him do. Especially since he sometimes did phone sales himself and knew how it felt to get hung up on.

I listened to Madeline as she strolled off, whistling an off-key verse of "Winter Wonderland."

I had a feeling her good mood was about to change.

Chapter 12

After Madeline left the barn, Catman scooted closer so Mason could reach the foal better.

"How about giving your horse a name, Mason?" I suggested.

Mason stayed quiet so long I was afraid he'd left us again. Then he wrinkled his pixie nose. "Mason?"

"Mason?"

"Far out!" Catman said.

But it was a bad idea. I, for one, couldn't take the confusion. "Well, that name's taken, Mason. Let's keep thinking, okay?"

He nodded and looked relieved. I couldn't force him to hurry any more than I could force the foal. I needed both of them to trust me.

We continued to rub the foal's head. Then we moved to her lips and mouth. "Get ready,"

I whispered. "We're going to feel her tongue. She'll probably suck our fingers, but that's just fine."

She did too. Mason shuddered, then giggled.

"Far out," Catman muttered. "Cool, little dude. This is so happening!"

We kept going, imprinting, stroking Friendly's mane and rib cage. "Mason, you're great at this!" I said. I wanted to hug him, but I didn't have a hand free.

Suddenly the barn door banged open, and we all jumped. I lost my grip on the foal, and she squirmed away. I couldn't let her get up. But I couldn't hold her either.

"Catman!" I pleaded.

But he was blocked by Mason, who was clinging to his neck.

The foal struggled to her feet and escaped to Nickers, who looked ready to fight off the enemy, whatever it was.

Madeline Edison stormed up to the stall, not even aware that she'd just ruined everything. "Mason, come here!"

Mason wouldn't let go of Catman.

The foal scurried to the far wall, with Nickers snorting beside her.

I got to my feet. "Madeline!" I shouted, until I remembered I'm not supposed to shout at adults. I bit my lip and made the words come through my teeth so they wouldn't sound so loud. "We were doing so great. You scared us."

"Well, I'm sorry, Winnie. I really am. But don't blame me. You can blame your father for being such a rude host."

When she said *father*, she made it sound like *FAH-ther*. She ventured into the stall, as if dodging land mines, reached down, and pulled Mason away from Catman.

Mason buried his head in her shoulder when she turned to leave.

"Wait! We weren't finished!" I shouted.

She kept going.

"When can he come back?" I hollered.

"You'll have to ask your *fah-ther!*" she shouted back as she raced out of the barn and stomped off toward her van.

I'd always hated it when Madeline called my dad "Jack." That's what my mom used to call him. But the way she was saying "your father" gave me goose bumps.

I turned back to Catman, who was already moving toward the paddock, probably to take up his watch for the North Star. "I better go see if Dad's okay."

Catman made the peace sign and disappeared behind the barn.

Peace. It felt as far away as the North Star.

I hurried to the house. "Lizzy?"

Lizzy came out of our room. "Boy, did you miss it, Winnie. Madeline finally showed."

"I know. What happened?"

Lizzy lowered her voice. "It was awful. Dad said Madeline didn't think of anyone but herself, that she thought *her* inventions were important, but that she wasn't even interested in his. Madeline denied it and said Dad wasn't understanding, that he should know how it is when you're on the verge of invention and you lose track of time, and she thought they knew each other well enough to—"

"Where is he?" I asked, interrupting.

"In the workshop. I feel terrible for both of them, Winnie. Dad ran straight out there. I'm making him broccoli lasagna. Maybe he'll talk to *you*."

I doubted it. Dad and I had to work at talking to each other, even when everything was going fine. But I had to try.

I found Dad hovered over his workbench, surrounded by golf balls in various stages of disaster. Some were charcoal black, others spotted brown, others cut open. The roar of the space heater made it hard to hear. Dad had on his orange work suit that's only in fashion on death row.

"Hey, Dad. How's it going?"

Dad swung around as if I'd surprised him. "Great! Never better."

I've never been good at making conversation with any human, especially with Dad. "So . . ." I tried hard to think of something safe to say. "That golf-ball thing sounds like a really great invention."

"That's what *I* thought, Winnie. Until I phoned the local golf course and was informed about Ohio golf courses' no-smoking policy. No more *smoking* golf buddy. It would have been helpful if a certain inventor could have brainstormed with me. But since I'm not important enough to waste a certain inventor's valuable time . . ."

"Um . . . Dad, you want to brainstorm with

me?" I suggested, worrying about the veins popping out on the sides of his forehead.

Dad glanced down at me, then took a deep breath. "Well, Winnie, as it happens, your dad didn't need anybody. No, sir. I solved this little glitch all on my own."

"That's great, Dad!" He hadn't needed Madeline after all. I figured this might be a good time to make my exit. "I guess I'll be going back to the barn then."

"Wait a minute, Winnie! Let me show you the new and improved golf buzzer buddy!" He sorted through the balls on his worktable and came up with a regular-looking golf ball, except for the wires. In one hand Dad held the ball and what looked like a remote control.

"Of course, I'll make the *real* golf buddy wireless. But this should give you the idea." He made a tiny golf club out of his finger and thumb and pretended to swing at the ball in his hand. "I tee off with a long drive that hooks deep into the rough off the fairway."

Dad tossed the ball with the others on the worktable. "Now, where is that ball? I know! I'll ask the golf buzzer buddy." He pressed the remote, and a horrible buzzer sounded.

I had to cover my ears. It was 10 times worse than the basketball buzzer at school. "Turn it off, Dad!" I begged. When he did, I uncovered my ears. "I thought golf was this big, quiet game with everybody shushing everybody else."

Dad stared at the remote in his palm. His face looked like all the bones had slipped down to his chin. "Golf *is* a quiet game with everybody shushing everybody," he admitted weakly.

I felt horrible. "Dad, what do *I* know? I can't tell a golf club from a tennis club!" I faked a laugh, but he didn't.

I backed toward the shop door, wishing I'd never even tried to cheer Dad up.

Note to self: Stick with horses.

Chapter 13

Catman was right where I thought he'd be
when I got back to the barn. He'd taken up his
spot in the paddock where he could see straight
through the *V* of the oak tree to the North Star.

I sat beside him and stared at it too.

"How's Mr. W.?" he asked.

"Worse since *I* talked to him."

I thought about Madeline standing Dad up,
and Sal standing *me* up, and Brian standing Sal
up, and Geri standing Lizzy up. "Why can't
people keep their word, Catman?"

Catman didn't answer, but I guess it wasn't a
real question. Instead he pointed to another part
of the sky. "M."

I didn't get it. "What?"

"M's favorite constellation, Cassiopeia. Looks like a squashed *M*."

I actually saw it, and it *did* look like someone had sat on an *M*.

The stars had poked through moving gray clouds, making the sky look layered.

"What time is it?" I asked. "Never mind. I forgot you never wear a watch."

"Don't need one," he said, surveying the sky. "The North Star is the center of the clock. It doesn't move. Earth does. Picture this, man! A line out through Dubhe and Merak, the pointers on the Dipper." He pointed them out. "That's your hour hand. Far out, huh?"

I tried to imagine a giant clock in the sky, with the North Star a dot in the middle. It wasn't that hard. "But isn't the hand between six and seven?"

"Right-on!" Catman exclaimed.

"But it can't be six-thirty."

"At midnight on March 1," he explained, "the hour hand points straight up. It moves backward. But each *hour* is two hours past midnight. So you have to subtract two hours for each month past March. You read it . . . about 6:30 A.M. Subtract two hours for each month past March 1 . . . let's say 10. Must be about 8:30 P.M."

"That was easy," I muttered. No wonder Catman got straight A's in math.

When Catman left for Barker's, I went back to the house. I was hoping Hawk would call. I wanted to tell her how well Friendly and Amigo had done today. And I wanted to know when she'd be home. Besides, it was fun to hear her talk about the party.

I'd finished my peanut-butter-and-cheese sandwich and was on my second cup of Lizzy's peanut-butter hot chocolate when Hawk called.

Right away I launched into an instant replay of the day. When I was done, I realized that Hawk hadn't said anything. "Sorry, Hawk. Tell me more about your party. Anything I can do? Maybe Lizzy can bake something? When will you be home, anyway?"

"That is actually why I am calling. I will not be home Sunday."

"Hawk! New Year's Eve is Monday night! What if your plane's late Monday? You can't show up late to your own New Year's Eve party!"

"Winnie, my father has already entered Towaco and me in the New Year's Day Appaloosa competition in Orlando. I will not be home until school starts." Her voice was flat, and she sounded like her mother.

I couldn't believe it. "But . . . but what about the party?"

I knew I sounded selfish. I *felt* selfish. This was just one more party to Hawk. But it was my only party. "That's not fair, Hawk! Tell your dad you want to come home!"

"I cannot hurt his feelings."

"Then call your mom. Let *her* tell him."

Hawk was quiet. I think I heard her sniffing. "They did talk. They had a horrible argument. I guess the separation agreement gave me to my father for the entire time."

Gave her to her father?

"I'm sorry, Hawk," I said. "I was being stupid. You and Towaco will knock 'em dead in the New Year's Day show. Bring back a huge trophy, okay?"

We hung up. Before I fell asleep, I prayed for Hawk. And for her parents.

Sunday morning Lizzy had green-frog pancakes waiting for Dad and me when we got up. But it made me sad because it's Geri who's crazy about frogs. And as far as I knew, Lizzy still hadn't heard from her.

We usually ride to church with the Barkers. But since the Barker Bus would have been too crowded with Granny Barker and Catman, Dad drove us in the cattle truck.

Ralph Evans is our substitute pastor. His real job is at the animal shelter, but he's a great pastor too. He was wearing khakis and a long-sleeved white shirt instead of his white animal-shelter jacket. Otherwise he was exactly the same Ralph.

This morning he talked about New Year's resolutions, making and breaking them. "God's not waiting to zap you if you don't keep your word," Ralph said. "You're not doing God any favors by making him big promises to last a whole year. Not that there's anything wrong with that. Goals are good. It's probably going to take *me* a whole year to lose my extra Christmas weight." He patted his stomach, and we all chuckled with him.

"But mostly, I think God wants us to be faithful in little things, one day at a time, just walking with Jesus."

I liked that. Being patient and peaceful a little bit at a time sounded a whole lot better than promising I'd be that way for a whole year.

"And if you blow it," Ralph continued, "you don't have to wait a whole year to make another resolution. Just tell God you're sorry. He'll be right there handy, ready to help. He won't let you down."

Ralph's smile faded. "On the other hand, I can almost guarantee that *someone* is going to let you down next year. And you're going to let someone down too. The good Lord knows we're human. But don't give up on each other. When someone lets you down, look past that friend you *can* see to that Friend you *can't* see. And you just keep on being faithful."

Since Ralph had semi-laryngitis this morning, his sermon wasn't as long as usual. Even though it was short, it was compact. Like a Falabella miniature horse—all there in a smaller size.

Ralph's last phrase bounced around my brain as we sang another hymn and shook each other's hands and walked outside. *"The Friend you can't see."* It was weird how Lizzy had said something to God almost like that, that God was her best friend.

As I climbed into the cattle truck, my mind was halfway into another on-the-spot prayer: *God, I know you're trying to tell me things or you wouldn't bother to have both Lizzy and Ralph talk about how you're their best friend. So, thanks. And help me get there too.*

On Sundays, when we ride home with the Barkers, everybody talks at once about the sermon. But in the cattle truck, none of us said a word until we were almost home.

I was thinking about what Ralph had said about not giving up on people. It sounded kind of like imprinting—not pulling away, even when the horse is trying to. I'd never had much luck with human friends. Maybe God was trying to tell me something about human friends too—about not giving up on *them*. But horses are so much easier to not give up on than humans.

Lizzy broke our silence. "I'm calling Geri as soon as we get home."

I started to warn her that she was asking to get her feelings hurt. But I stopped. I had a feeling Lizzy already knew that.

Lizzy was on the phone before she changed out of her church clothes.

I changed into jeans and a sweatshirt. And when I walked back into the kitchen, Lizzy was pulling out the flour and sugar from the cupboard.

"Well?" I asked. "What did Geri say?"

"She said she'd be over as soon as she finished lunch," Lizzy answered.

"Well, don't get your hopes up," I warned. "Sal said *she* was coming over after church too. But I'm not holding my breath."

It was a good thing I didn't hold my breath for Sal. By midafternoon, she still hadn't come.

Geri showed up, though. I watched from the barn as her mom dropped her off and waited until Geri reached the porch and the door opened.

I was glad for Lizzy. I just wished Sal had come too.

I hung out with the horses most of the afternoon. Friendly let me stroke her all over while she nursed from Annie. I took Nickers and Friendly into the paddock for some fresh air. Amigo was already coming around. He followed when I led him, and he didn't try to bite me anymore. I had to get Sal to spend time with him and see what a great friend Amigo could be for her.

Around four o'clock, I went in for something to eat and was hit with the smell of ginger cookies. I'd been all set to be mad at Geri. But when I saw her with Lizzy, giggling over gingerbread geckos, my anger fizzled.

"Hey, Lizzy. Geri," I called, shrugging out of my coat. "Smells great in here."

Lizzy smiled at me, then put her finger over her lips and pointed to Dad. He was punching in numbers on the kitchen phone.

I joined Lizzy and Geri and eavesdropped.

"Hello, Madeline?" he said, his voice cracking.

We three girls leaned forward, as if that could help us hear what Madeline was saying. She must have said a lot because Dad didn't say anything for a full minute.

When Dad did speak again, he had his regular voice back. "I know. Me too. So, do you want to come over?"

Again we leaned closer, nobody breathing.

"That would be great!" Dad said. He hung up, grinning.

In spite of myself I was grinning too.

Dad was whistling as he headed for his workshop. Lizzy and Geri were giggling over the geckos.

I walked over to the phone and stared at it. Maybe I should call Sal. It had worked for Lizzy and Dad. I'd try to be nice, just like they were. Patient. Peaceful. I dialed the number.

"Hello, Mrs. Cracker?" I turned my head away from the receiver and cleared my throat. "This is Winnie Willis. Is Sal there?"

"Salena?" she asked. She shouted away from the phone, "Nathan! Where is your sister?"

I could hear Nathan in the background, but I couldn't make out what he was saying.

Gram Cracker came back on the line. "She's tanning at Tanfastic with that Spidell girl."

"With Summer?" All my patience and peace evaporated. "Sal's with Summer?"

"They're probably talking about that girl's— Summer's—big New Year's Eve party. All night they tied up the phone talking about it."

So Summer was taking over and having the party Hawk was supposed to have. And that meant Winnie Willis was back where she belonged . . . on the outside looking in.

I gripped the phone, imagining Summer and Sal laughing and making plans, inviting every-body in our class except me. Until that minute I don't think I'd realized how much I'd wanted to be included, to have a real New Year's Eve party to go to.

"Why are you calling?" Gram Cracker demanded. "Is something wrong with that little creature?"

It took me a second to realize she was talking about Amigo. "Amigo? No! He's doing great. Really he is. That's why I was calling. Sal was supposed to come over and help. Amigo and Sal could be friends if she'd give him a chance."

"Salena was supposed to go over there?" Mrs. Cracker's voice got an edge to it. "Nathan talked both of us into leaving the horse with you for a while. Does his sister think I am made of money? That I can just pay that pony's upkeep until she gets around to doing whatever she should be doing with it? I'll send her to you the moment she returns."

When I hung up, I wasn't grinning like Dad and Lizzy had. I didn't think Sal was going to appreciate me getting her in trouble with her grandmother.

It was almost suppertime when Gram Cracker dropped Sal off at my barn. Except for her earmuffs and a feathery jacket that looked like 100 birds had died to make it, Sal looked like she was just in from Daytona Beach. Her face was reddish brown, almost as bright as her hair.

"Sorry I'm late, Winnie." At least she didn't sound mad.

"That's okay. We don't have much daylight left, but the barn lights should work."

I led Sal toward Amigo's end stall, but she stopped to look at Nickers, the foal, and Annie.

"I can't believe you got it to nurse from that goat!" she exclaimed. "That is so tight!"

We watched the foal for a while, even though I knew the last minutes of good daylight were slipping away. I starting thinking about Sal's mom and dad and wondering why I'd never seen them at school, even though Hawk said they both lived in Ashland.

"When are your parents coming back, Sal?" I asked.

She shrugged. Then she kind of huffed a hard laugh. "It's a good thing my mom's out of town. Yesterday Gram picked up the mail and opened a letter from school. *Another* note from Treadwater."

Mr. Treadwater is our math teacher. He's short, with a face that would fit right in on Mount Rushmore. He's pretty boring, but he loves numbers so much you have to like him.

Sal continued. "I intercepted the first note a couple of weeks ago: 'Salena is often rebellious and disrespectful. We hope to see improvement next semester. Signed, C. Treadwater.'" Sal did a pretty good impression of him, making her voice flat and bland. "So, of course, I threw that one away. Then I wrote one of my own to his wife: 'Mr. Treadwater is often dull and boring. We hope to see improvement next semester.'"

"Sal!"

"Yeah. He wrote back. And that's the note Gram opened. But she's cool. She probably won't even give it to Mom."

I couldn't even imagine what my dad would do if I pulled something like that.

Amigo pawed from his stall.

"You sure that horse is tame now?" Sal asked.

"I didn't say that," I admitted. "But he's better. He just needs to know he can trust you."

We moved down to Amigo's stall. He turned his back on us but let me walk up to him. I led him over to Sal. "See how calm his eyes look?" The white rim of fear around his pupils had vanished, and his neck was relaxed.

Until he saw Sal. He stopped short and laid back his ears. I hoped Sal didn't read horse language. Amigo definitely didn't trust her.

I scratched his chest and felt him relax again.

Sal eyed the Falabella. She's so tall that Amigo's head didn't come to her waist. "So what am I supposed to do with it?" she asked, taking a step backward. "I can't ride it. Are you positive it won't grow?"

I moved my fingers to the sides of Amigo's mouth and got him to open for me. "His baby teeth are gone. He's got a full mouth, but no Galvayne's groove. That's the deep groove on a horse's upper incisor. It shows up at about 10 years old. I'd say Amigo's about five. He's done growing."

"Great," Sal muttered sarcastically.

It took a lot of coaxing, more for Sal than for Amigo, but finally Sal was able to at least pat her horse. It wasn't much, but it was a start.

"We've got time for a short imprinting lesson, Sal. It will help you and Amigo bond."

She looked skeptical, but she didn't bolt from the barn. Mom believed in imprinting, or at least touching, nervous horses no matter how old they were. She said it was good for the horse and good for the owner.

"I hear a car," Sal said, pulling her hand away and trying to peer up the stallway.

"It's probably just Madeline."

Sal started to come back to Amigo, but there was the sound of another car outside, louder than the first one. The engine raced.

"Is your dad having a party or something?" Sal asked.

"Nope." Whoever it was, I hoped they'd stay out of the barn. Sal was so close to giving Amigo a try.

Amigo looked up with his big doe eyes. How could anybody even think about sending him away?

Snow crunched. The barn floor creaked.

"Who's there?" I called.

"There you are!" Summer Spidell came down the stallway, watching every step as if I'd laid land mines for her, which, I admit, was sounding like not so bad of an idea.

"Summer!" Sal called, leaving her horse . . . and me. "How did you know I was here?"

"I called about napkin colors. I can't decide without you. Your grandmother said you'd be here."

Summer has dozens of horses at her stable. She owns the most expensive horse in the county, maybe in all Ohio. Her dad's Stable-Mart costs a zillion times more than my barn. All she ever does is make fun of me *and* my barn. Why couldn't she just stay at her own place?

"Look, Summer. Sal and I are in the middle of something here. Do you mind?" I knew I sounded like Summer usually did, mean and snotty. But I'd had it with her.

"What?" she asked, all innocent-like.

"Stop it, Summer! We all know why you came by tonight."

"My goodness, Winifred," she said, glancing at Sal, like she didn't know what to say to crazy Winnie. "Why do you think I came by?"

"To horn in! To drag Sal away again. To mess up my life more than you already *have* messed it up!"

Amigo trotted away from me. I stopped talking. I was so angry I was shaking.

Summer turned her big blue eyes and pouty lips on Sal. "I don't understand. I just came by to invite Winifred to my New Year's Eve party."

"Right," I said. No way Summer Spidell would invite *me* to her party.

"Don't you want to come?" Summer asked, faking hurt.

"Sure . . . ," I said, waiting, expecting the axe to fall. For Summer to laugh at the idea of me at her house, her party.

"Good then," Summer said. "It's settled. Tomorrow night at seven. Don't be late." She was taking this too far.

"Maybe Lizzy can make candy or cookies," Sal suggested.

Summer whirled around on her. "Mother has it all catered, and—" she stopped herself, took a breath, then turned back to me—"that would be . . . nice . . . if your sister wants to."

I frowned at Summer. "Let me get this straight. *You* are inviting *me* to your New Year's Eve party."

She smiled, and if I hadn't known her so well, I would have bought it. She was that good.

"So when I show up tomorrow night at seven, nobody's going to call the police? No water balloons?"

Summer laughed. "It's New Year's Eve, not April Fool's Day."

"It'll be so tight, Winnie!" Sal said. "Tons of guys are coming. Brian's having his brother drive us and everything."

Summer smiled sweetly again.

I couldn't trust Summer. On the other hand, Sal had heard her invite me. It would be pretty hard to uninvite me.

"You really want me there?" I asked, one more time.

"Of course we do!" Summer said.

"Okay then. Thanks." *I* was going to Summer Spidell's party?

"Now," Summer said, checking her watch, "if we're going to be ready in time, I really do need Sal's help. We have to decorate tonight. Do you mind, Winnie?"

I *did* mind. Amigo was too important to put off for any party, even a real New Year's Eve party. "I don't know, Summer. Sal needs time with her horse."

"Could she do it tomorrow instead?" Summer asked.

Sal shivered and hiked up her red boots. "I'll come at 11. For real, Winnie. If I don't, you can come over to Gram's and drag me out by my hair."

What could I say? They were going to work on a party *I'd* just been invited to.

"It's a deal. Go. But be here by 11 or I'll take you up on that dragging you out by your hair offer, Sal!" But I was already talking to the wind.

Lizzy and Geri couldn't believe it when I told them Summer had invited me to her party. But I still had to ask Dad.

Dad was in his easy chair, with Madeline sitting on the broad arm of the chair, even though the whole couch was going to waste. I started to remind Dad about the no-sitting-on-the-chair-arm rule, but I didn't want to spoil his mood before he gave me his permission to go to the party.

"Sure. You can go," Dad said when I asked him. "But we'll miss you here, Winnie. Madeline and Mason are coming over to welcome in the new year." He turned to Geri. "You'll come too, won't you, Geri?"

"I'll ask Mom, but I'm sure it will be okay. Thanks, Mr. Willis," Geri said.

"I'll be glad to help you with your hair, Winnie," Madeline offered.

"Thanks," I said, wondering how much help that would be. Hair isn't one of her best features.

"I'm sorry about the way I stormed the barn yesterday, Winnie," she said. "Mason said I scared that little colt."

I didn't think this would be the right time to correct her. *Colts* are males. *Fillies* are females.

"That's okay," I said. "Mason and the foal were awesome, though. Right, buddy?"

I said the last part louder because, since I'd come inside, Mason had been sitting cross-legged beside the old couch, staring unblinking at the armrest. He's fascinated with splotches, and I think I'd spilled root beer there about 100 years ago (when the couch was only 50).

Mason grinned over at me. I was relieved he hadn't gone off somewhere in his head.

Madeline brushed something off Dad's sleeve. "So what did you name that colt?"

"That's Mason's job," I answered, winking at him. "He's still going over all his options."

They stayed for Lizzy's spaghetti and pepperoni. Then we popped popcorn. And finally it was time for them to go.

"Do you think you could bring Mason over tomorrow morning?" I asked as they moved toward the door. "I'd love to get him together with his filly again."

"I want to pet my filly," Mason said as plain as day. He's like 10 different people, and you never know which of them will speak up. I love them all.

I reached down and ruffled his wispy hair, making it stand up with static electricity.

Lizzy helped Mason with his coat. "But you

have to come early, Mason," she said, "because Winnie is going to a big party and has to get all dressed up, like Cinderella at the ball."

Mason stared up at me through his thick glasses. "Are you famous?"

I shook my head. "If you only knew, Mason."

But after they left, I did feel kind of famous. Not really. But not totally unpopular, at least. I was going to a real New Year's Eve party. Summer herself had invited me.

Note to self: Life is a mystery.

Dad and Lizzy went to bed, but I waited for Hawk to call. She wouldn't believe that Summer had actually invited me to her party. But I knew she'd be happy for me.

When the phone rang, I got it before the first ring was over. "Hawk?"

"Winnie!" Hawk sounded excited too. "Did Summer ask you to her party yet? She better have asked you. It's the only way I said she could take over my party and have it at her house. My mother wanted to have the party as soon as I get home. But I told Summer *she* could have the New Year's Eve party . . . as long as she invited Winnie Willis."

Note to self: Mystery solved.

I thought about it most of the night. Summer had only invited me to her party because Hawk made her. Twice I got out of bed for a better look at Catman's star. It was there, shining right where it had been every night. Something about that made me feel better.

Dad was still asleep when I got up, but Lizzy and Geri weren't around. I figured they were prowling the snowy fields in search of creatures in distress.

I grabbed a banana for breakfast and had to take off its pointy hat and ribbon tie, ignoring the raisin eyes, before I could eat it. Lizzy and Geri had decorated the whole bowl of fruit.

Alone, all my midnight thoughts came back. So Summer Spidell didn't invite me of her own free will. So what? I could still have a great time. Hawk wouldn't be there, but other kids in my class were kind of nice. Like Kaylee, who sits by me in a couple of classes and always greets me with a smile. She'd get invited. And Grant. He was okay.

It was still a New Year's Eve party, and I was going.

The door burst open, and Lizzy and Geri stormed in.

"There she is!" Geri shouted. "Wait 'til you see what we got!"

Lizzy set a brown grocery bag on the table. "Sweet! But before you look, Winnie, just know that we're not done with it yet."

I wasn't all that anxious for a look. I've seen the things Lizzy drags home—cockroaches, spiders, snakes.

"Go ahead! Open it!" Geri commanded.

I lifted the bag. Too light for a snake. Too heavy for a roach.

I opened the bag and peeked in. A big black

piece of material was folded in the bottom. I pulled it out. It was a long, shimmery, black skirt, the same kind of cool material Summer wears.

"Lizzy found it at Goodwill! Can you believe it?" Geri sounded amazed.

It was perfect. Simple but fancy. Something a famous person would wear. "Thanks, you guys. I love it."

"You have to try it on. I'll take up the hem, but it's your size," Lizzy said.

I'm so short that Lizzy has to hem everything she gets for me. "I hadn't even thought about what I'd wear. How dumb is that?"

"I think she really likes it," Geri whispered to Lizzy.

"I do! I love it." But I was starting to wonder what I could wear with it. I mostly had sweatshirts and T-shirts and a couple of sweaters that were warm, but not fancy. And two dresses for church.

"What's the matter?" Geri asked.

I forced a smile. "Nothing. I'm just . . . trying to decide what I'll wear with it."

"We've already thought of that!" Lizzy exclaimed. "Go on, Geri! Show her!"

Geri set *her* white plastic bag on the table.

"Now, this was mine. But I only wore it once. Then I got a growth spurt, and the sleeves got too short. My mom was so excited somebody might get some use out of it. My grandmother gave it to me for—"

"Just give it to her!" Lizzy urged.

Geri pulled out a white blouse. But not just any old blouse. It might have been silk. The sleeves ended in a ruffle at the wrist. It had a high collar and tiny pearl buttons.

"Thanks, Geri."

I tried on everything. The blouse fit great, and Lizzy pinned up the skirt. They even argued about how I should wear my hair and whether or not I could wear lipstick.

The morning kept getting better. Madeline brought Mason over as promised. And he was in the best mood. We spent a whole hour with the foal, doing all the imprinting with the filly standing beside Nickers. I don't think I'd ever seen Mason so happy.

We finished before 11, when Sal was supposed to come. About a minute after

Madeline and Mason drove off, I heard another vehicle drive up.

Sal! Right on time.

But the *ba-ru-ga* of the horn told me it was the Barker Bus.

I ran out to meet them. Barker and Catman piled out of the van. Granny and Mrs. Barker were in the front seat.

"You should be proud of Annie, Granny B," I told her. "That goat has been letting the foal nurse all she wants."

Granny Barker looked like she'd had her head stuck out the window on the drive over. Her snow-white hair framed her face like a cloud. "That's the good Lord's way."

The rest of the van was filled with Barker's brothers and their dogs. Mrs. Barker let all of them come to the barn to see the filly. Mark carried Zorro, but the other boys had to leave their dogs in their doggy seat belts. Barker had each dog so well trained, though, that there wasn't a single bark out of them the whole time we were in the barn.

Finally Mrs. Barker rounded up her boys. "Eddy," she called, as she started the Barker Bus again, "we'll come back for you and Catman after we pick up groceries for tonight. Bye, Winnie! Happy New Year, in case I don't see you!"

"Happy New Year, Mrs. Barker!"

Catman and Barker played with the foal while I cleaned Amigo's stall. I kept listening for Sal to come, but she didn't.

"What time is it, Barker?" I asked when I finished mucking.

"High noon," he answered.

Sal was an hour late. "I can't believe Sal is doing this to me again," I complained. "Every day she says she'll come over. Then she doesn't."

Barker looked sympathetic, but he didn't say anything. He'd never say something bad about anybody.

Friendly nudged Catman, who pretended to tumble down. Then the filly sidled over to Annie and started nursing.

I pictured Sal the day before, giving me her word that she'd be over at 11. "You know," I said slowly, as the words came back to me, "Sal told me herself that if she didn't show up today, I could go over and drag her out of bed. I think I'll take her up on that offer!"

Two minutes later, I was galloping Nickers through the snow. I'd left Barker and Catman in charge of the barn. But the filly was so intent on getting her lunch from Annie that she didn't even fuss when I sneaked Nickers out.

I could tell Nickers was worried, though. Her muscles tensed, and she snorted with the wind as we crossed the pasture toward the other side of town. We would have made even better time, but a light snow began to fall, bringing a white fog.

With every *thump* of Nickers' hooves, I grew angrier and angrier at Sal. Did she think I didn't have anything better to do than sit around and wait for her? *I* was going to the same party *she* was. I had things to do too. I had a life.

Well, I wasn't going to let her get away with standing me up again.

By the time Nickers pulled up in front of the little house at the far edge of Ashland, I was fuming. "Stay," I told Nickers, sliding off her back into the snow.

I knocked harder than I needed to on the old, splintered door.

Nathan opened it. "Winnie? What are you doing here? Is that your horse?"

"Can I come in, Nathan?"

"Sure. Gram isn't here, though. We're going to a party across the street. At Slick Hair's. That's what Sal calls him. I don't really want to go."

I felt sorry for Nathan. He wasn't a bad kid. "When will your parents be back?" I asked.

The TV was blaring from the living room, which might have been smaller than ours and didn't have Lizzy to clean it. Nathan turned off the TV, and I followed him in.

"Who knows when my parents will be back? We didn't even know they were leaving." He plopped on the striped couch and let the newspapers fall to the floor.

"What do you mean, Nathan?" I sat down with him.

"Well, we never know when Dad comes or goes. Not since he got married again."

"Your dad got remarried?" I wondered if Hawk knew.

"Yeah. He's got a little baby even. A boy. He's pretty cute. I saw him right after he was born, but they wouldn't let me hold him. Andrew. That's his name."

I couldn't imagine my dad remarrying and moving away and having a baby named Andrew. "What about your mom?"

"I think she thought we were spending Christmas break with Dad. The first day school got out, we went over there for one night. The next day, Dad said they were going to Ellen's parents' in Pennsylvania, I think. Sal was still asleep, so Dad said we could go back to Mom's whenever we wanted to. He even left money for a taxi."

"So what happened?"

Nathan shrugged. "We took the taxi back, but Mom wasn't there. Sal said she'd gone off some-where for a vacation with Beer Belly. That's what Sal calls him. We stayed there by ourselves for two days until we ran out of food and I called Gram Cracker. Sal was so mad she didn't speak to me, not even on Christmas Day."

From the roof came a sound like glass break-ing. Sleet . . . or hail.

"I'm sorry, Nathan." Lizzy would have known exactly what to say, but I didn't.

We sat there for a minute. "Hey, Nathan. I never got to thank you for talking your grand-mother into giving me a chance with Amigo.

He's doing great. You should come over and see him."

"Okay."

We were quiet another minute. Then I asked, "Is Sal still asleep?"

"Huh-uh."

"Is she still in her bedroom?"

"Uh-huh."

"So will you go get her for me?"

Nathan shook his head hard. "Huh-uh."

"Nathan! Why not?"

"Too scary. I heard her yelling and went up to see what was wrong. She threw her boot at me." He pointed to his arm, but I couldn't see anything. "She got me. See?"

I stood up. "Which room is hers?"

"She doesn't have a room. She's in Gram's. Second door on the left. Good luck. It's been nice knowing you, Winnie Willis."

170

I moved down the hall, flanked on both sides by velvet pictures of kids with hollow eyes. A cigarette smell grew stronger.

Cautiously I knocked on Sal's door.

Something struck the door from the other side. It sounded like Sal's other boot.

"Go away!" she shouted.

I shot up a quick prayer because Sal sounded pretty mad.

"Sal, it's me. Winnie. You said I could drag you out by your hair if you didn't show up." I tried a fake laugh, but I'm no Summer. It came out a gurgle.

The door opened, and Sal stuck her head out. Her eyes were as red as her hair, which had two new green streaks. "I forgot," she said, looking

171

behind me, as if she thought I'd come with a posse.

"It's not too late," I said, checking to see if she had anything in her hand that she might throw at me. "We could ride back to the barn now."

Sal sniffed. She dabbed at her eyes with a shredded Kleenex. "All right."

All right? Just like that? I'm not sure what I expected, but this wasn't it.

If I'd been Lizzy, I would have gone inside Sal's room and said just the right thing that would have made Sal open up and spill out everything that was wrong.

Instead I said, "Let's go."

Sal pulled a bright pink ski jacket out of the closet. I'd never seen her wear it, and I suspected it was Gram Cracker's.

"Nathan," Sal said at the door, "Gram should be back any minute to go to that party with you. So be ready. You okay here?"

"I'm okay." To me, he whispered, "Be careful. And watch your back."

We went outside. Sleet was falling in slanted sheets.

Nickers, glistening wet, did a little rear, then came trotting to me.

"That's our ride?" Sal asked.

I jumped on first and then showed Sal how to use the front step to climb on behind me.

She's so tall, it wasn't hard for her to mount. But once she got on, she gripped so hard around my waist that I could barely breathe.

"Winnie, I've never been on a horse before!"

"Never?"

"Never!"

"Then why were you so upset that you couldn't ride Amigo?" I asked.

"I wasn't," she admitted.

Nickers took off toward home at a fast walk. I kept her to a walk until Sal loosened her grip. Then I skipped the trot and urged Nickers into a lope.

"Winnie!" Sal cried.

"Relax, Sal!" I had to shout above the wind that swept across us, pelting us with tiny pieces of ice. My cheeks felt like they were being stuck with tiny pins. "Just go with the motion. Smooth as a rocking chair."

Sal buried her head in my back, but her grip let up.

I prayed that God would make me more like Lizzy and give me the right words for Sal. After a couple of minutes of silence I blurted out, "Sal, why were you crying? Are you sad about something?"

"Wow!" she said. "You guessed it. I *am* sad. Winnie, you should be a psychologist."

Sal can be pretty sarcastic when she wants to be.

After a couple of seconds she said, "I'm sorry, Winnie. It's just . . . Brian called and broke up with me."

To be honest, I thought breaking up with a boy seemed about as dumb as going with one. I still didn't get it, the way girls in my class claimed they were *going out* with a guy, but they never went anywhere. I could care less myself. But I didn't say this to Sal. I'm not that dumb.

"Sorry, Sal. He sure acted like he was crazy about you."

"Brian is a jerk," she said. "I, Salena Fry, do hereby make the following New Year's resolution: I will give up men!"

I thought 12 years old was kind of young to give up on men, especially since *I* hadn't even started hoping for them yet. But maybe in Sal's case it wasn't such a bad idea.

"Good for you!" I said.

"Yeah! Good for me!" she said even louder. "Guys! Who needs them?"

We cantered back through the pastures while ice battered us. Nickers' steady breathing sounded regular and loud. Sal held on tight, but I heard her laugh behind me.

The Barker Bus was waiting in front of the barn when we rode up. Catman and Barker hadn't wanted to leave until I got back. I thanked them, and they hurried to the yellow van.

"Catman's cool," Sal said after we were alone. "Barker too."

"Yep."

Sal and I went to the house to change into dry clothes. Lizzy donated a pair of her sweat pants and a sweatshirt, since all my stuff was way too small on Sal.

"Hey, at least I don't have to worry about Brian seeing me in this getup," Sal said, checking herself out in the mirror. It definitely wasn't her usual look.

When we came into the kitchen, Lizzy had hot chocolate and salamander cookies waiting. We dug in.

"These are the best cookies I've ever eaten, Lizzy," Sal said.

"Geri helped with this batch." Lizzy elbowed her friend. "She got a really cool salamander for Christmas. Want to see it? She brought it over."

"I'll pass," Sal said, downing another cookie. "Man, Nathan is right. You really are the best baker in town."

I glanced at Geri to see if she minded. But she kept grinning.

Dad walked in from the workshop. "Did you guys start the party without me?" He wiped his forehead with his sleeve. "Sal, right? How are you?"

Sal looked surprised that Dad remembered her. "Okay. How are you, Mr. Willis?"

"Not bad, as it happens." Dad pulled a slightly singed golf ball from his pocket. Wires ran all over it. From his other pocket he pulled a tiny black box.

"What is it?" Sal asked.

"Don't ask," I whispered.

"Glad you asked!" Dad said. "It's the chipmunk golf buddy!"

"Doesn't look much like a chipmunk," Sal observed.

"Ah . . . but look *and* listen."

"Dad, we really better get to the barn and—"

"Go ahead, Mr. Willis," Sal said, ignoring me. "What's a chipmunk golf buddy?"

Dad filled Sal in on the history of the golf buddy, through the entire smoking-buddy stage, past the buzzer stage, and ending with the contraption in his hand.

"So you see, I had to have an *ordinary* sound that wouldn't disturb the other golfers but would still let the owner of the golf buddy find his ball. Check this out." Dad set the ball on the table, flipped the switch on the remote, and the ball went *chit, chit, chit, chit.*

"That sounds just like a chipmunk!" Sal exclaimed. "How did you do that?"

Dad actually blushed. "Well, I have a long way to go. I'll make it wireless, of course. And I can't add weight to the ball."

"It must be so tight to be an inventor," Sal said. "What else are you working on?"

"Funny you should ask, Sal," Dad said. "Just this morning, I got the idea for an alarm squirter. You know? For those mornings when you sleep right through the radio *and* the buzzer. The clock would squirt you with water."

"Man! I'd cut my tardies in half if I had something like that. Can I see it?" Sal asked.

"I've only just started . . . but sure! Come on!"

It was unbelievable. Sal followed Dad to his workshop and stayed there for 30 minutes.

Finally I had to go out and get her. She was down on her knees, holding a piece of clear plastic tubing while Dad attacked his old alarm clock.

"We're almost there, Winnie!" Dad called. "Sal has a good eye for invention."

Sal grinned at me.

I let them play awhile longer, then dragged Sal out to the barn.

Outside, it had stopped sleeting. But the rain had frozen on tree branches, wrapping them in clear, sparkling ice. The trees twinkled.

Amigo was ready for us. This time everything was different between Sal and him. Sal wasn't in a rush. And Amigo didn't try to bolt from her. We did a whole imprinting session, just like Mason and I had done with the filly. Winnie the Horse Gentler was back. Nickers could go back to just being Nickers.

"He's not such a bad little guy, is he?" Sal said, scratching Amigo's chest. "Wouldn't he look tight in pierced earrings?"

"Not a good idea." I showed her the horse greeting, how to blow into her horse's nostrils. Sal tried it. It took her three attempts before Amigo blew back. When he did, Sal acted as if he'd recited the Gettysburg Address.

"He'll be a great friend for you, Sal. You could keep him in your grandmother's backyard. There's room enough. He'll be easy to take care of."

Please, God. Please?

"Maybe you're right," Sal said.

Thank you!

"I had a really good time, Winnie," Sal said, as if that fact had taken her totally by surprise.

"Me too. But we better get a move on, Sal. I have to wash my hair and get ready. I'm sure you do too. Dad can drive you home. Oh, yeah. Brian won't come to get you. Dad's dropping me off. We could swing over and pick you up first and maybe—"

"Winnie," Sal interrupted. "Brian will be there. No way I'm going to that party."

Sal and I made our way up to the house. The clouds were breaking apart and letting patchy light through, turning glazed branches into giant diamonds.

"If you don't go to Summer's party, what will you do, Sal?" I asked. "Is it too late to go with your grandmother and Nathan?"

"Yeah, thank goodness. Gotta admit, I hate being at Gram's by myself. That place is creepy at night, but it's better than Slick Hair's."

I rode along when Dad drove Sal to Gram Cracker's. We scrunched in the cab of the cattle truck, and Sal didn't even make a wisecrack about our only "car."

"Are you all set for the big night?" Dad asked, obviously trying to make conversation.

"I don't plan to do much," Sal said, focusing out the frosted window that reminded me of Granny B's doilies.

"Aren't you going to the Spidell New Year's Eve party?" Dad asked.

"Nah. I'll probably crash early. Or maybe I'll catch a horror flick on TV."

Dad tried to get me to look at him, but I stared straight ahead. It wasn't *my* fault Sal wasn't going to Summer's party. She could go. So what if Brian was there?

"Well, why don't you come over and celebrate with us?" Dad offered. "Madeline's coming over. And Lizzy and Geri have cooked up enough for an army."

In the reflection of the windowpane I caught a glimpse of Sal's face. I thought I saw her eyes flicker, then go out.

"No. That's okay, Mr. Willis. But thanks. I'd feel weird."

"We'd love to have you," Dad insisted. "Are you sure, Sal?"

"I'm sure."

Dad pulled up in front of the Cracker house, and Sal hopped out.

"Winnie," she said before she shut the cab door, "be cool." She smiled at Dad. "Thanks for the ride and everything, Mr. Willis."

She bumped the truck door shut, then walked toward the house.

Dad didn't pull away.

My stomach felt like harness horses were racing in it. I kept imagining Sal in that house, alone, watching a horror movie. Crying.

I leaned across and threw open the door. "Sal! Come back!"

Sal turned around, frowning.

"Come back!" I shouted. "I'm not going to that party either."

Sal retraced her steps, still scowling. "I thought you said you *were* going."

"You know me. I'm not big on parties. Come on. We'll celebrate with Amigo and Nickers and the foal. How's that?"

"And *me!*" Dad added.

"And the slightly crazy Willis clan," I agreed.

Sal grinned. "Yeah?" She shrugged. "I was kind of looking forward to that horror flick . . . but okay."

"Good. Get in," I said.

Sal shook her head. "Need to change first. And a hot bath. It's stopped storming. I'll just walk over later."

"Won't hear of it," Dad insisted. "How's this? I'll drop Winnie back home. She can use a shower herself. Then I'll pick up Madeline and Mason and swing back over here for you. Maybe in an hour? Will that work?"

"Cool." This time Sal trotted to the house and waved before going inside.

I'd like to say that I felt great and was looking forward to greeting in the new year more than ever. But I didn't feel great. I'd probably never get invited to another New Year's Eve party. For sure, not one of Summer's parties.

Dad dropped me off at home, and I went straight to the phone and dialed Summer's number. I had to look it up. It's not like Summer and I are phone buddies.

The phone rang four times before someone picked up. "Hello?" It was a guy's voice. Young. But not Richard.

"I'm sorry. I was trying to call Spidells'."

"Winnie? Is that you?"

"Grant?"

"Yeah. I got roped into setting up tables. You wouldn't believe it over here. Summer and her mom have gone crazy decorating. Hey, do you have a way to get here? We could get somebody to give you a lift. It's still pretty wicked out there. You don't want to walk."

"I'm not coming." My stupid voice cracked.

"You're not? I thought Summer said you were."

"I was. That's why I'm calling. Things have changed. So I won't be there."

"Why, Winnie?" Grant sounded like he really wanted to know. Like it mattered.

So I told him. Maybe I shouldn't have, but it all came out. About Sal. About Brian. About how I'd decided to stay so Sal wouldn't end up alone at her grandmother's house.

"Well, I'm sorry you won't be here, Winnie." He sounded like he meant it. "Sal's lucky to have you for a friend." In the background I heard Summer shouting and someone else laughing. "I've got to go," Grant said. "Happy New Year, Winnie."

He hung up before I could wish him the same. But I guess *he* didn't need it.

I hung up and saw Lizzy and Geri staring at me.

"That was a really good thing you did, Winnie," Lizzy said. "You're a good friend."

"And Lizzy knows everything about being a good friend," Geri added. "Must run in the family."

"Come on," Lizzy said, taking my hand, "let's get you ready for *our* party!"

By the time we heard Dad's truck pull up, we were all ready. Lizzy and Geri wore matching black stretch pants and frog-green shirts, and I wore my *famous* skirt and blouse.

Mason came thundering into the house first, looking like a miniature orchestra conductor in a black suit and tie, which he wriggled out of before he reached the kitchen. "New Year!" he shouted. "New Year!"

I lifted him up and swung him around. "New Year to you too, Mason!"

Dad was taking Madeline's coat.

I peered behind them. "Where's Sal? Dad! Did you forget to pick her up?" It would be so like my dad.

I caught a glance between Madeline and Dad. Then she said, "I'll go see if I can help Lizzy in the kitchen."

Dad finished hanging up their coats, then turned to me. "Sal wasn't there, Winnie."

"What do you mean she wasn't there?"

"I honked. I knocked. I even prowled around the house and peeked in windows, against my better judgment. Madeline insisted. But nobody was home."

"But she *had* to be there!"

"Look," Dad said. "Maybe she just stepped out to a neighbor's or something. Or maybe she started walking over."

But I could tell he didn't believe that any more than I did.

I called Sal, but nobody answered. How could she do that? I slammed the receiver. I'd never speak to Sal again—not that she'd notice. It wasn't fair. I'd done what Lizzy and Dad did with their *friends*. I'd been there for Sal, even when she'd showed up hours, or a whole day, late. And where had it gotten me?

Here. While everyone else in my class was at Summer's.

For the next hour I ate Lizzy's cookies and tried to act like I was having a good time. I even ate one of Madeline's sandwiches. She'd brought them over in her battery-powered bun warmer, which had overheated and nearly fried the tuna.

I thought Sal might at least call me and let me know where she'd gone. I even rehearsed what I'd say to her, how I'd tell her off. But the phone just hung there on the wall, not ringing once.

"Would you like me to run over and see if your friend's home now, Winnie?" Madeline offered.

I shook my head. "Thanks for asking, though."

I waited until Mason fell asleep on the couch. Then I made my escape for the barn.

But before I reached the front door Lizzy caught me. "Here." She handed me a small bag that smelled like molasses. "I made these treats for the horses. I'm sorry about Sal, Winnie."

"Well, don't be," I snapped. *"I'm not."*

A few stars peeked around night clouds as I walked to the barn, but I couldn't see the North Star, no matter how hard I looked.

Nickers greeted me as soon as I stepped inside the barn. I slipped into the stall with Nickers and Friendly and breathed in the smell of hay and horse as if I'd swum up from deep water and needed oxygen.

"Hey, guys," I said, putting one arm around each of them. "Nice to be with creatures I can count on." I gave them Lizzy's homemade treats that looked like everything horses love held together with molasses. Nickers gobbled hers down, and Friendly lipped hers and nibbled some of the oats. Lizzy had even made one for Annie Goat.

Amigo came up when I went into his stall. And for the first time he nickered to me. Then he downed his treat in two bites.

After a while the horses went back to their hay nets, and I moved outside to the paddock. I pulled out a bale of hay and sat on that, leaning against the barn. I still couldn't see Catman's North Star, even when I looked through the V of the tree.

"Winnie?" Lizzy called from the barn.

Maybe Sal had finally called. "Out here, Lizzy!"

She came out, hugging her arms and shivering. I could tell by her expression that she didn't bring good news.

"Sal didn't call, huh?" I said.

"No. But Hawk did. She tried to call you at Summer's to wish you Happy New Year. She wants you to call her tomorrow. She was on her dad's cell."

"Is that all, Lizzy?"

"No. Nate called to wish us Happy New Year. Winnie, he said Sal and Brian are back together. They went to Summer's party. I'm so sorry."

Big, fat surprise.

I didn't say anything. I couldn't. So this was how the old year would end and the new year begin.

Come on inside, Winnie," Lizzy urged. "In a half hour it will be the new year."

"I'll be in pretty soon, Lizzy."

She tried to talk me into coming with her. Finally she gave up and ran back to the house.

I opened the stalls and let Amigo into the paddock. Nickers pushed open her stall door, and she and Friendly trotted out too. The three of them pranced around the paddock. I knew those horses, and they'd come to trust me.

If Sal were a horse, I'd have had a chance of understanding her. *So how come everything works with horses, and nothing works with humans?* I asked God.

I sat on the bale, stared up at the sky, and tried to imagine what Summer and Sal and my classmates were doing at that exact moment. Then I tried to imagine what was going on in Sal's head. That's what I'd done with Amigo. I do it with all horses. I try to think like they do.

Sal probably needed to feel a part of Summer's crowd, to believe she had a boyfriend. She didn't have a Lizzy. Her dad didn't sound like my dad. I didn't think she had Jesus as a friend either. But she still didn't have to act so tough around me, like she didn't even care that I gave up the party for her.

The branches creaked inside their icy shells like they wanted out. Sal had a pretty hard shell. I wondered if she ever wanted out. Lizzy told me once that bugs have their skeletons on the outside. The hard outside protects their soft insides. Maybe that's how it was with Sal.

I felt someone behind me. "Lizzy?" I turned around.

But it wasn't Lizzy. Sal stepped out of the barn. She was wearing the pink ski jacket, with a red miniskirt and red high heels.

An hour ago I might have yelled at her and told her off. But without my even knowing when it happened, the yelling had gone out of me. "What are you doing here, Sal?"

She sat next to me on the bale and emptied snow out of her shoes. "What do you mean? I *said* I was coming, didn't I?"

"Right."

Amigo trotted by us. I thought of how far that horse had come.

"Grant told me that you probably *did* want to go to the party, that you just canceled so I wouldn't spend New Year's Eve alone." Sal stared at her hands as if she couldn't figure out where the fingers came from, like they belonged to someone else.

Something inside me thawed, and I wondered if this is what peace feels like.

"Nobody's ever done anything like that for me, Winnie. Just kept being there for me. You know?" Sal elbowed me. "I haven't been the most reliable horse-training partner in the world."

I grinned up at her. Her eyes glistened like the iced trees. "Sal, are you crying?"

She swiped her eyes with her pink sleeve. "Me? No way! And don't think this means we're buddies or anything."

"Us? No way!" I said, but I didn't mean it.

"Still," Sal said, "it's pretty tight that you gave up that party for me."

Amigo walked up to Sal and stretched out his neck to be scratched. Sal obliged him.

"Far out!"

Catman Coolidge strolled out of the barn, followed by Barker and a host of cats.

"Catman? Barker?" I cried. "I can't believe you're *here!*"

"We already cheered in the new year at my house," Barker said. "We pretended nine o'clock was midnight. That way Johnny, Mark, Luke, and William got to stay up. Matthew's still up. But Catman and I thought we'd hike over and wish you Happy New Year."

"I'm glad you did." And I couldn't have thought of two people I'd rather start out the new year with.

"Pull up a bale," Sal said.

Catman and Barker dragged out another bale of hay and took their seats.

We stared silently at the stars for a minute. All kinds of things were swirling in my head. Good thoughts, though—about patience and peace, about imprinting and how maybe that's the way Jesus was working with me, staying with me even when I struggle. And how maybe that's how I'm supposed to work with other people.

The sky was beautiful, even with clouds hiding half the stars. "The only thing we need is that North Star of yours, Catman," I complained. "Wish it were still up there."

"It's groovy, man," Catman assured me. "The star is always there, whether you see it or not."

Of course! That star had been there all the time, even when I couldn't see it. I thought about what Ralph had said, about Jesus always being there, about the friend you see and the Friend you don't. God had been there all the time too, even when I hadn't seen him.

Then the whole crew thundered through the barn and came into the paddock. Lizzy and Geri led the way, carrying platters covered with foil.

"We've got food!" Lizzy shouted.

"Do we ever!" Geri said. "Toasted cheese-and-peanut-butter sandwiches and french fries, complete with a jar of mayonnaise for fry dipping!"

Mason stumbled out into the paddock. He slipped on an icy patch but caught himself and kept barreling straight for the foal. Then he stopped and walked slowly up to her.

I glanced back at Madeline. She looked like she was biting her lip clear through so she wouldn't freak out over Mason and the foal. But she didn't yell or call him back.

The filly let Mason put his little arms around her neck.

"Hi, buddy," Mason muttered. *"My* buddy."

"That's a great name for her, Mason!" I called. So what if *Buddy* was more of a boy's name. The foal *was* Mason's buddy. It was perfect.

Nickers whinnied loud and long. As we all looked over at her, she buckled her knees and dropped into the snow. Then my horse rolled to her side. Up to her knees. Back to her side. Then she rolled over on her back and wiggled, side to side, making deep shapes in the purple-patterned snow.

Amigo plopped into the snow and mimicked Nickers. Then Buddy did the same thing.

"Great idea, Nickers!" I shouted, running out beside her. "Snow angels!"

I let myself free-fall backward, arms outstretched, landing in the snow with a crunch, but sinking below the crusty surface to the soft snow beneath.

All around me I heard the *crunch, plop, thud* as Catman and Barker and Sal dropped like stones into the snow next to me. Then Lizzy and Geri and Mason. And even Dad and Madeline.

"Happy New Year!" Sal hollered.

And we all shouted the same thing.

We swung our arms and legs, making snow angels, sinking deeper into the silence of the snow. Trees held their breath. The only sounds were Nickers' contented grunts, the foal's whinny, and the *swish, swish* of snow angels.

I gazed up at a star I couldn't see but knew was there. And I thanked God for a new year, knowing that no matter what it might bring, God would be there with it, in every moment, sure as the North Star.

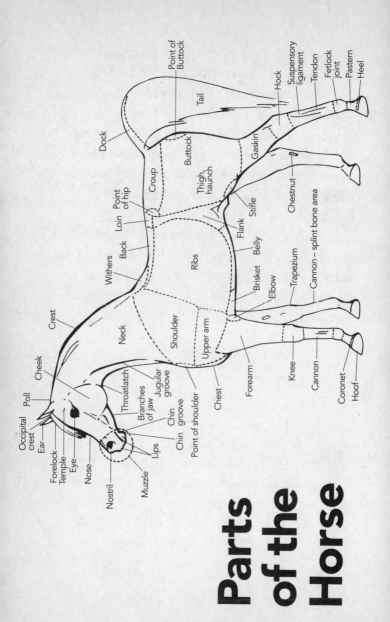

Parts of the Horse

🐎 Horse Talk!

Horses communicate with one another . . . and with us, if we learn to read their cues. Here are some of the main ways a horse talks:

Whinny—A loud, long horse call that can be heard from a half mile away. Horses often whinny back and forth.
Possible translations: Is that you over there? Hello! I'm over here! See me? I heard you! What's going on?

Neigh—To most horse people, a neigh is the same as a whinny. Some people call any vocalization from a horse a neigh.

Nicker—The friendliest horse greeting in the world. A nicker is a low sound made in the throat, sometimes rumbling. Horses use it as a warm greeting for another horse or a trusted person. A horse owner might hear a nicker at feeding time.
Possible translations: Welcome back! Good to see you. I missed you. Hey there! Come on over. Got anything good to eat?

Snort—This sounds like your snort, only much louder and more fluttering. It's a hard exhale, with the air being forced out through the nostrils.

Possible translations: Look out! Something's wrong out there! Yikes! What's that?

Blow—Usually one huge exhale, like a snort, but in a large burst of wind.

Possible translations: What's going on? Things aren't so bad. Such is life.

Squeal—This high-pitched cry that sounds a bit like a scream can be heard a hundred yards away.

Possible translations: Don't you dare! Stop it! I'm warning you! I've had it—I mean it! That hurts!

Grunts, groans, sighs, sniffs—Horses make a variety of sounds. Some grunts and groans mean nothing more than boredom. Others are natural outgrowths of exercise.

★★★★★

Horses also communicate without making a sound. You'll need to observe each horse and tune in to the individual translations, but here are some possible versions of nonverbal horse talk:

EARS

Flat back ears—When a horse pins back its ears, pay attention and beware! If the ears go back slightly, the horse may just be irritated. The closer the ears are pressed back to the skull, the angrier the horse.

Possible translations: I don't like that buzzing fly. You're making me mad! I'm warning you! You try that, and I'll make you wish you hadn't!

Pricked forward, stiff ears—Ears stiffly forward usually mean a horse is on the alert. Something ahead has captured its attention.

Possible translations: What's that? Did you hear that? I want to know what that is! Forward ears may also say, I'm cool and proud of it!

Relaxed, loosely forward ears—When a horse is content, listening to sounds all around, ears relax, tilting loosely forward.

Possible translations: It's a fine day, not too bad at all. Nothin' new out here.

Uneven ears—When a horse swivels one ear up and one ear back, it's just paying attention to the surroundings.

Possible translations: Sigh. So, anything interesting going on yet?

Stiff, twitching ears—If a horse twitches stiff ears, flicking them fast (in combination with overall body tension), be on guard! This horse may be terrified and ready to bolt.

Possible translations: Yikes! I'm outta here! Run for the hills!

Airplane ears—Ears lopped to the sides usually means the horse is bored or tired.

Possible translations: Nothing ever happens around here. So, what's next already? Bor-ing.

Droopy ears—When a horse's ears sag and droop to the sides, it may just be sleepy, or it might be in pain.

Possible translations: Yawn . . . I am so sleepy. I could sure use some shut-eye. I don't feel so good. It really hurts.

TAIL

Tail switches hard and fast—An intensely angry horse will switch its tail hard enough to hurt anyone foolhardy enough to stand within striking distance. The tail flies side to side and maybe up and down as well.

Possible translations: I've had it, I tell you! Enough is enough! Stand back and get out of my way!

Tail held high—A horse who holds its tail high may be proud to be a horse!

Possible translations: Get a load of me! Hey! Look how gorgeous I am! I'm so amazing that I just may hightail it out of here!

Clamped-down tail—Fear can make a horse clamp its tail to its rump.

Possible translations: I don't like this; it's scary. What are they going to do to me? Can't somebody help me?

Pointed tail swat—One sharp, well-aimed swat of the tail could mean something hurts there.
Possible translations: Ouch! That hurts! Got that pesky fly.

OTHER SIGNALS

Pay attention to other body language. Stamping a hoof may mean impatience or eagerness to get going. A rear hoof raised slightly off the ground might be a sign of irritation. The same hoof raised, but relaxed, may signal sleepiness. When a horse is angry, the muscles tense, back stiffens, and the eyes flash, showing extra white of the eyeballs. One anxious horse may balk, standing stone still and stiff legged. Another horse just as anxious may dance sideways or paw the ground. A horse in pain might swing its head backward toward the pain, toss its head, shiver, or try to rub or nibble the sore spot. Sick horses tend to lower their heads and look dull, listless, and unresponsive.

As you attempt to communicate with your horse and understand what he or she is saying, remember that different horses may use the same sound or signal, but mean different things. One horse may flatten her ears in anger, while another horse lays back his ears to listen to a rider. Each horse has his or her own language, and it's up to you to understand.

🐎 Horse-O-Pedia

Akhal Teke—A small, compact horse with an elegant head. The Akhal Teke, also known as Turkmen, is fast, strong, and reliable—a great, all-around riding horse.

American Saddlebred (or American Saddle Horse)—A showy breed of horse with five gaits (walk, trot, canter, and two extras). They are usually high-spirited, often high-strung; mainly seen in horse shows.

Andalusian—A breed of horse originating in Spain, strong and striking in appearance. They have been used in dressage, as parade horses, in the bullring, and even for herding cattle.

Appaloosa—Horse with mottled skin and a pattern of spots, such as a solid white or brown with oblong, dark spots behind the withers. They're usually good all-around horses.

Arabian—Believed to be the oldest breed or one of the oldest. Arabians are thought by many to be the most beautiful of all horses. They are characterized by a small head, large eyes, refined build, silky mane and tail, and often high spirits.

Barb—North African desert horse.

Bay—A horse with a mahogany or deep brown to reddish-brown color and a black mane and tail.

Blind-age—Without revealing age.

Buck—To thrust out the back legs, kicking off the ground.

Buckskin—Tan or grayish-yellow-colored horse with black mane and tail.

Caballero—A Spanish or Latin horseman. A cowboy.

Camargue—A tough, surefooted, but high-stepping and beautiful horse native to southern France. Camargues have inspirited artists and poets down through the centuries.

Cannon—The bone in a horse's leg that runs from the knee to the fetlock.

Canter—A rolling-gait with a three time pace slower than a gallop. The rhythm falls with the right hind foot, then the left hind and right fore simultaneously, then the left fore followed by a period of suspension when all feet are off the ground.

Cattle-pony stop—Sudden, sliding stop with drastically bent haunches and rear legs; the type of stop a cutting, or cowboy, horse might make to round up cattle.

Chestnut—A horse with a coat colored golden yellow to dark brown, sometimes the color of bays, but with same-color mane and tail.

Cloverleaf—The three-cornered racing pattern followed in many barrel races; so named because the circles around each barrel resemble the three petals on a clover leaf.

Clydesdale—A very large and heavy draft breed. Clydesdales have been used for many kinds of work, from towing barges along canals, to plowing fields, to hauling heavy loads in wagons.

Colic—A digestive disorder in horses, accompanied by severe abdominal pain.

Colostrum—First milk. The first milk that comes from a mare contains the antibodies the foal needs to prevent disease.

Conformation—The overall structure of a horse; the way his parts fit together. Good conformation in a horse means that horse is solidly built, with straight legs and well-proportioned features.

Crop—A small whip sometimes used by riders.

Cross-ties—Two straps coming from opposite walls of the stallway. They hook onto a horse's halter for easier grooming.

Curb—A single-bar bit with a curve in the middle and shanks and a curb chain to provide leverage in a horse's mouth.

Dapple—A color effect that looks splotchy. A dapple-gray horse will be light gray, covered with rings of darker gray.

D ring—The D-shaped, metal ring on the side of a horse's halter.

Dutch Friesian—A stocky, large European breed of horses who have characteristically bushy manes.

English Riding—The style of riding English or Eastern or Saddle Seat, on a flat saddle that's lighter and leaner than a Western saddle. English riding is seen in three-gaited and five-gaited Saddle Horse classes in horse shows. In competition, the rider posts at the trot and wears a formal riding habit.

Falabella—The smallest horse in the world, a miniature horse rather than a pony, standing less than 34 inches, usually 20–32 inches. Falabellas were first seen in herds of Mapuche Indians of Argentina and first bred by the Falabella family.

Founder—A condition, also known as laminitis, in which the hoof becomes deformed due to poor blood circulation. Major causes are getting too much of spring's first grass, overeating, drinking cold water immediately after exercise, excessive stress, or other ailments.

Frog—The soft, V-shaped section on the underside of a horse's hoof.

Gait—Set manner in which a horse moves. Horses have four natural gaits: the walk, the trot or jog, the canter or lope, and the gallop. Other gaits have been learned or are characteristic to certain breeds: pace, amble, slow gait, rack, running walk, etc.

Galvayne's Groove—The groove on the surface of a horse's upper incisor. The length of the Galvayne's groove is a good way to determine a horse's age.

Gelding—An altered male horse.

Hackamore—A bridle with no bit, often used for training Western horses.

Hackney—A high-stepping harness horse driven in showrings. Hackneys used to pull carriages in everyday life.

Halter—Basic device of straps or rope fitting around a horse's head and behind the ears. Halters are used to lead or tie up a horse.

Hand or **Hands high**—The unit of measure to describe a horse's height. A hand equals four inches (10 cm). Horses are said to be a certain number of "hands high."

Hay net—A net or open bag that can be filled with hay and hung in a stall. Hay nets provide an alternate method of feeding hay to horses.

Headshy—Touchy around the head. Horses that are headshy may jerk their heads away when someone attempts to stroke their heads or to bridle them.

Heaves—A disease that makes it hard for the horse to breathe. Heaves in horses is similar to asthma in humans.

Hippotherapy—A specialty area of therapeutic horse riding that has been used to help patients with neurological disorders, movement dysfunctions, and other disabilities. Hippotherapy is a medical treatment given by a specially trained physical therapist.

Horse Therapy—A form of treatment where the patient is encouraged to form a partnership with the therapy horse.

Hunter—A horse used primarily for hunt riding. Hunter is a type, not a distinct breed. Many hunters are bred in Ireland, Britain, and the U.S.

Imprinting—A learning process, generally referring to gentling a newborn foal, in which a behavior pattern is established and the foal bonds with a human. The foal is touched and handled in much the same way a mare would nuzzle her foal.

Leadrope—A rope with a hook on one end to attach to a horse's halter for leading or tying the horse.

Leads—The act of a horse galloping in such a way as to balance his body, leading with one side or the other. In a *right lead*, the right foreleg leaves the ground last and seems to reach out farther. In a *left lead*, the horse reaches out farther with the left foreleg, usually when galloping counterclockwise.

Lipizzaner—Strong, stately horse used in the famous Spanish Riding School of Vienna. Lipizzaners are born black and turn gray or white.

Lunge line (longe line)—A very long lead line or rope, used for exercising a horse from the ground. A hook at one end of the line is attached to the horse's halter, and the horse is encouraged to move in a circle around the handler.

Lusitano—Large, agile, noble breed of horse from Portugal. They're known as the mounts of bullfighters.

Manipur—A pony bred in Manipur, India. Descended from the wild Mongolian horse, the Manipur was the original polo pony.

Mare—Female horse.

Maremmano—A classical Greek warhorse descended from sixteenth-century Spain. It was the preferred mount of the Italian cowboy.

Martingale—A strap run from the girth, between a horse's forelegs, and up to the reins or noseband of the bridle. The martingale restricts a horse's head movements.

Miniature or **Mini**—A unique breed of horse that is an elegant, scaled-down version of the large-size horse. Miniature horses can't be taller than 34 inches.

Morgan—A compact, solidly built breed of horse with muscular shoulders. Morgans are usually reliable, trustworthy horses.

Mustang—Originally, a small, hardy Spanish horse turned loose in the wilds. Mustangs still run wild in protected parts of the U.S. They are suspicious of humans, tough, hard to train, but quick and able horses.

Paddock—Fenced area near a stable or barn; smaller than a pasture. It's often used for training and working horses.

Paint—A spotted horse with Quarter Horse or Thoroughbred bloodlines. The American Paint Horse Association registers only those horses with Paint, Quarter Horse, or Thoroughbred registration papers.

Palomino—Cream-colored or golden horse with a silver or white mane and tail.

Palouse—Native American people who inhabited the Washington–Oregon area. They were highly skilled in horse training and are credited with developing the Appaloosas.

Percheron—A heavy, hardy breed of horse with a good disposition. Percherons have been used as elegant draft horses, pulling royal coaches. They've also been good workhorses on farms. Thousands of Percherons from America served as warhorses during World War I.

Peruvian Paso—A smooth and steady horse with a weird gait that's kind of like swimming. *Paso* means "step"; the Peruvian Paso can step out at 16 MPH without giving the rider a bumpy ride.

Pinto—Spotted horse, brown and white or black and white. Refers only to color. The Pinto Horse Association registers any spotted horse or pony.

Poll—The highest part of a horse's head, right between the ears.

Post—A riding technique in English horsemanship. The rider posts to a rising trot, lifting slightly out of the saddle and back down, in coordination with the horse's bounciest gait, the trot.

Presentation—The way the foal comes out at birth. Normal presentation is for a foal to have two front hooves appear, followed by the nose between the legs.

Przewalski—Perhaps the oldest breed of primitive horse. Also known as the Mongolian Wild Horse, the Przewalski Horse looks primitive, with a large head and a short, broad body.

Quarter Horse—A muscular "cowboy" horse reminiscent of the Old West. The Quarter Horse got its name from the fact that it can outrun other horses over the quarter mile. Quarter Horses are usually easygoing and good-natured.

Quirt—A short-handled rawhide whip sometimes used by riders.

Rear—To suddenly lift both front legs into the air and stand only on the back legs.

Roan—The color of a horse when white hairs mix with the basic coat of black, brown, chestnut, or gray.

Snaffle—A single bar bit, often jointed, or "broken" in the middle, with no shank. Snaffle bits are generally considered less punishing than curbed bits.

Sorrel—Used to describe a horse that's reddish (usually reddish-brown) in color.

Spur—A short metal spike or spiked wheel that straps

to the heel of a rider's boots. Spurs are used to urge the horse on faster.

Stallion—An unaltered male horse.

Standardbred—A breed of horse heavier than the Thoroughbred, but similar in type. Standardbreds have a calm temperament and are used in harness racing.

Stifle—The joint between the thigh and the gaskin—the hip joint.

Surcingle—A type of cinch used to hold a saddle, blanket, or a pack to a horse. The surcingle looks like a wide belt.

Tack—Horse equipment (saddles, bridles, halters, etc.).

Tarpan—A hardy, native breed of pony that survived on the tough terrain of Russia, the Carpathian Mountains, and the Ukraine. The original Tarpan is extinct, but a related breed exists in Poland.

Tennessee Walker—A gaited horse, with a running walk—half walk and half trot. Tennessee Walking Horses are generally steady and reliable, very comfortable to ride.

Thoroughbred—The fastest breed of horse in the world, they are used as racing horses. Thoroughbreds are often high-strung.

Thrush—An infection in the V-shaped frog of a horse's foot. Thrush can be caused by a horse's standing in a dirty stall or wet pasture.

Tie short—Tying the rope with little or no slack to prevent movement from the horse.

Trakehner—Strong, dependable, agile horse that can do it all—show, dressage, jump, harness.

Turnout time—Time a horse spends outside a barn or stable, "turned out" to exercise or roam in a pasture.

Twitch—A device some horsemen use to make a horse go where it doesn't want to go. A rope noose loops around the upper lip. The loop is attached to what looks like a bat, and the bat is twisted, tightening the noose around the horse's muzzle until he gives in.

Waxing—The formation of thick drops of first milk that begin leaking from a mare's udders. It may look like honey or wax.

Welsh Cob—A breed of pony brought to the U.S. from the United Kingdom. Welsh Cobs are great all-around ponies.

Western Riding—The style of riding as cowboys of the Old West rode, as ranchers have ridden, with a traditional Western saddle, heavy, deep-seated, with a raised saddle horn. Trail riding and pleasure riding are generally Western; more relaxed than English riding.

Wind sucking—The bad, and often dangerous, habit of some stabled horses to chew on fence or stall wood and suck in air.

🐎 Author Talk

Dandi Daley Mackall grew up riding horses, taking her first solo bareback ride when she was three. Her best friends were Sugar, a Pinto; Misty, probably a Morgan; and Towaco, an Appaloosa; along with Ash Bill, a Quarter Horse; Rocket, a buckskin; Angel, the colt; Butch, anybody's guess; Lancer and Cindy, American Saddlebreds; and Moby, a white Quarter Horse. Dandi and husband, Joe; daughters, Jen and Katy; and son, Dan (when forced) enjoy riding Cheyenne, their Paint. Dandi has written books for all ages, including Little Blessings books, Degrees of Guilt: *Kyra's Story,* Degrees of Betrayal: *Sierra's Story, Love Rules,* and *Maggie's Story.* Her books (about 400 titles) have sold more than 4 million copies. She writes and rides from rural Ohio.

Visit Dandi at www.dandibooks.com

Winnie
The Horse Gentler

COLLECT ALL EIGHT BOOKS!

CP0015-B

Winnie
The Horse Gentler

Can't get enough of Winnie? Visit her Web site to read more about Winnie and her friends plus all about their horses.

IT'S ALL ON WINNIETHEHORSEGENTLER.COM

There are so many fun and cool things to do on Winnie's Web site; here are just a few:

⭐ PAT'S PETS

Post your favorite photo of your pet and tell us a fun story about them

⭐ ASK WINNIE

Here's your chance to ask Winnie questions about your horse

⭐ MANE ATTRACTION

Meet Dandi and her horse, Chestnut!

⭐ THE BARNYARD

Here's your chance to share your thoughts with others

⭐ AND MUCH MORE!